ENEMIES WITH CONSEQUENCES

MICHELLE SMART

PRESENTS

Recycling programs for this product may not exist in your area.

ISBN-13: 978-1-335-21381-5

Enemies with Consequences

Harlequin Enterprises ULC
22 Adelaide St. West, 41st Floor
Toronto, Ontario M5H 4E3, Canada
www.Harlequin.com

HarperCollins Publishers
Macken House, 39/40 Mayor Street Upper,
Dublin 1, D01 C9W8, Ireland
www.HarperCollins.com

Printed in Lithuania

"Open the door right now or I'll break it down."

Close to tears, she choked out, "*Go away.*"

"Last chance. Open it, *now*."

Marnie knew better than anyone that Domenico never made idle threats. She'd known him since she was a month shy of her nineteenth birthday, had worked closely with him for six years and been married to him for one. If he said he'd break the door down, then he'd break the door down.

It took all her strength to lift her arm and turn the lock.

He swung the door open and gazed down at her.

A wave of misery hit her so hard and so fast.

She'd adored this man. Worshipped him. Would have done anything for him.

There was no mockery in the light brown stare. "You're ill."

She shook her head and wished that she'd turned around and gone home. She'd never wanted to tell him like this. In her head, she'd been standing tall, fully in control, ready to take whatever came next, not feeling more vulnerable than she'd ever felt before.

"Not ill," she whispered. "Pregnant."

Michelle Smart's love affair with books started when she was a baby and would cuddle them in her cot. A voracious reader of all genres, she found her love of romance established when she stumbled across her first Harlequin book at the age of twelve. She's been reading them—and writing them—ever since. Michelle lives in Northamptonshire, England, with her husband and two young smarties.

Books by Michelle Smart

Harlequin Presents

Christmas Baby with Her Ultra-Rich Boss
Cinderella's One-Night Baby
Resisting the Bossy Billionaire
Spaniard's Shock Heirs
Marriage Made in Revenge

The Greek Groom Swap

The Forbidden Greek

The Diamond Club

Heir Ultimatum

Greek Rivals

Forgotten Greek Proposal
His Pregnant Enemy Bride
Greek Boss to Hate

Visit the Author Profile page
at Harlequin.com for more titles.

ENEMIES WITH CONSEQUENCES

CHAPTER ONE

MARNIE WARE ENDED the call from her solicitor with shaking hands.

The marriage she'd entered with the wildly unrealistic dream of a fairy-tale ending was over. She was officially divorced.

Covering her mouth, she frantically swallowed back a swell of nausea that felt much different to the sickness that had been plaguing her for days and staggered back to the bathroom, the only vaguely cool room in the tiny flat she'd spent all but one year of her life in. A ray of mocking sunlight shone on the white stick she'd left upside down on the sink. By the time she psyched herself up to turn it over, her whole body was trembling.

Her chin was wobbling before she'd dared look at the window on the stick.

Two pink lines.

Sinking to the floor, Marnie hugged her knees to her chest and burst into tears.

Domenico Cannavaro ended the call from his divorce lawyer and closed his eyes.

Failure, he'd learned since his wife had left him,

tasted bitter. And now she was no longer his wife. She was now officially his ex-wife. That she was his second wife, specially chosen for the role thanks to her unswerving loyalty and devotion to him, along with her compliant, meek and mild manner, made the bitter taste especially acrid.

His mousy little wife, a woman who wouldn't say boo to a goose (if that was the correct English saying) had got her way and severed herself from him. She'd dumped his surname the same day she'd had the temerity to dump him. It still made him incredulous to remember how he'd gone out of his way to take her out for dinner to celebrate their first wedding anniversary, presented her with a beautiful bracelet chosen with great care by his PA, and been handed divorce papers in return. Galling didn't begin to describe how that had felt.

To think this was a woman he'd talent-spotted working the reception desk of his English branch as an eighteen-year-old, promoted onto his personal team and then promoted numerous more times until she reached the dizzying height of his PA, and then, all those years later, promoted to wife! This was the thanks he got for plucking her out of obscurity and nurturing her career and then giving her the most lavish lifestyle any woman could wish for? He was well rid of her.

Forget failure and bitterness; this called for a celebration. Not just any old celebration, a party.

Lifting the receiver on his desk phone, he summoned his latest PA.

Janie was in his office in a flash, all buxom, busty

beauty with tumbling, glossy black hair. The contrast between her and Domenico's wife could not be greater, in both looks and demeanour.

'I want you to call the usual caterers and have a buffet for two hundred people delivered to my home by seven this evening,' he ordered. He didn't need to tell her to order the best stuff. 'Champagne too. Crates of it. Cocktails. A full bar. And call that DJ we used for the staff summer party. Tell him to set up in the basement.'

Janie didn't bat an eyelid. 'All this for tonight?'

'Yes.'

'No problem. Anything else?'

'Let Washington know I won't be flying over tomorrow, and reschedule all my appointments. I'll fly over on Sunday.'

'On it.' She tilted her head and made the coquettish sweep of her eyelashes she'd adopted in recent months. 'Are you celebrating anything special?'

'Indeed I am, Janie. My divorce.'

She raised a perfectly plucked eyebrow and smiled. 'Congratulations.'

'Thank you.'

She made no effort to leave. 'Shall I attend the party to make sure everything runs smoothly?'

He didn't let his smile drop. 'That won't be necessary.'

She sidled to the door and swept her eyelashes at him again. 'I'll keep myself available in case you change your mind.'

'That's very thoughtful, but you enjoy your evening… Close the door on your way out.'

The moment the door was shut, Domenico dropped his smile and grimaced. Since it had become common knowledge that he and Marnie had split up, Janie had dropped more than a few hints that she would be a willing replacement. While she was an excellent PA, he had no desire to make her anything more, but her subtle flirtations were an excellent reminder that he was now officially free to flirt and sleep with whomever he wanted. His six-month celibacy had been broken only once during a night of madness he would give anything to eradicate from his memories, and it was time to throw himself back into the dating scene and enjoy his newfound freedom.

He hoped Marnie choked on hers.

Marnie got out of the cab and stared through the electric gates at the magnificent three-storey mansion she'd walked out of six months ago. An abundance of cars was parked on the sprawling driveway. It seemed like every light was on.

To her surprise, her fingerprint still worked to open the gate, which was just as well as Domenico was ignoring her calls. Which wasn't a surprise, not after the way things had ended the last time they'd seen each other. That had been exactly six weeks ago, the day their decree nisi had come through.

She didn't like to remember that night. Especially didn't like to remember the morning after. She'd practically thrown Dom out of the flat she'd moved back into after she'd left him. His parting shot had been a cruel, 'One day you'll wake up and look around this shithole, and it will hit you; everything you threw away.' His light brown eyes had been dark with anger. '*You* threw it away, Marnie. Remember that. You did it.'

She'd shut the door in his face without responding.

She would never regret her decision to end their marriage, and while the flat she'd moved back into seemed impossibly dingy and tiny compared to the luxury she'd lived in as Domenico's wife, there was comfort in the familiar. In any case, the settlement she'd accepted had meant that moving into something bigger was impossible.

He'd expected her to fight over the paltry settlement. A man worth billions could expect to hand over a decent chunk of his fortune in the event of divorce, even after only a year of marriage, but Marnie had taken the derisory lump sum offered in his opening gambit. Her solicitor had been horrified, the sum being equivalent to two years of the salary she'd been on before quitting—not through choice—her role as his PA for the much more exclusive role of his wife.

She hadn't wanted his money. She hadn't wanted to fight him—she *hated* fights, always retreated inside herself at the first sign of confrontation. All she'd ever wanted from Domenico was the one thing he would never give her. The one thing she'd spent her life craving.

The closer she walked to the house, the more attuned her ears became to the music vibrating through the walls. He was throwing a party. Celebrating the end of them. Why he should celebrate being rid of a wife he'd cared nothing for was a mystery she no longer cared to solve. None of the fights he'd tried to engineer after she'd left him or his general crappy behaviour over the divorce had been because he felt anything for her. Domenico just hated losing.

Marnie's love for him had died a death of a thousand cuts of his indifference.

She pressed her finger to the doorbell and willed the nausea to stay away for a little longer while she had the conversation she couldn't delay. As much as she hated Domenico, he deserved to know now, not later, and this was the first time that day she'd felt well enough to leave her flat and make the trek across London.

When no answer came, she placed her hand flat on the security lock and was again surprised to find the door opened for her. She'd assumed all her security clearance had been voided the day she walked out.

The noise blaring out explained why none of the staff had heard the bell. It was deafening, not just the music but the screams of laughter floating up from the basement.

Uncaring that she was wearing a floaty, pale green everyday summer dress and flat Roman sandals while the female guests milling around on the ground floor were dressed in all their high-heeled party finery, Marnie didn't allow any eye contact as she passed curious stares at her appearance and slipped down the stairs to the basement.

Domenico's basement was a party room. He loved entertaining. All his many homes had a dedicated entertaining room, and this, his London one, was his gaudiest, the one most designed for partying rather than corporate entertaining. When she'd still been his PA, she'd been expected to attend all his parties and functions to ensure everything went smoothly, and she prayed her replacement, Janie, wasn't one of the many bodies glittering under the strobes of the disco balls on the dance floor. Janie had once been Marnie's junior, a beautiful, vivacious creature who'd made her feel even more insignificant than she usually did. In Janie's presence, she felt as invisible as she had as a child.

As well as the people boogying on the dance floor, other bodies were taking a breather on the plentiful plump sofas. There were many faces she recognised. Most of them. Make that all of them. Domenico's friends and acquaintances. Marnie had always felt invisible amongst them, had been too shy to make any of them friends of her own. Invisibility could have been her superpower.

She didn't feel invisible now. Over the pulsing music, eyes began to clock her and widen with the same surprise she'd felt when finding herself able to enter the grounds and then the house.

One of the last people to notice her presence was the tall man in the centre of the dance floor, letting loose to the disco beat with a group of beautiful, scantily clad women. Almost a head taller than everyone else, his back was to Marnie, and she saw him bend his neck and cup his ear to hear what one of the women was saying to him.

He turned, bemusement on his face…bemusement that faded when he met Marnie's stare across the vast room.

As much as she wished it didn't, her heart twisted

painfully, and for a moment, the tiniest moment, everyone vanished, leaving only her and Domenico.

She would never forget the first time she'd set eyes on him. She'd only been working on the reception desk of Cannavaro Law International for three days when he'd strolled through the revolving door with his entourage. She'd guessed from the way all the female staff had been acting in the hour before his arrival, constantly checking their compacts and touching up their lipstick and fluffing their hair, that he was good-looking, but she'd been wholly unprepared for just *how* good-looking he was. Still only eighteen and living in her childhood bedroom with walls covered in posters of the pop stars and film stars she wanted to marry, Marnie would have gladly ripped them all down and plastered the walls with posters of him.

All the lawyers at the firm wore business suits, and all wore them like armour. Domenico wore his in an almost ironical way, his clothing and the artful messiness of his dark brown hair giving the air of a man happy to conform to the niceties of the business world, but only under his own terms. He'd been clean-shaven then, the goatee he'd adopted coming a few years later.

He'd strolled past the reception desk with generic greetings to the staff, clocked Marnie, and backed up.

'You're new,' he'd stated. His English contained barely a trace of accent.

Tongue-tied at his power and utter gorgeousness, she'd nodded.

Light brown eyes glittering with friendliness, he'd held out a hand. 'I'm Domenico.'

Cheeks flaming with embarrassment at being singled out, she'd reached over to take it and found her hand engulfed in his huge paw. 'Marnie,' she'd practically stuttered.

'Great to meet you, Marnie. How are you enjoying the job?'

She'd fought her shyness to say, 'Better now I've mastered the switchboard.' The switchboard didn't just link all the staff in the London offices; it connected with all the staff worldwide, and as Cannavaro International was one of the world's largest corporate law firms, that meant staff of thousands.

He'd pulled an impressed face. 'Already? Good for you.'

By the time he'd headed into the elevator to take him up to his penthouse office, Marnie had been smitten.

Now, the sensuous mouth she'd spent years dreaming of kissing hers tightened, and then his neck extended, his gorgeous features loosened, and the tall, lithe body currently wrapped in a silver shirt and black jeans wound its way towards her. The glittering in the light brown eyes was the glitter of menace.

By his own admission, Domenico had drunk more than was good for him. Much more. He didn't care. He'd earned the right to the coming hangover and had made sure to clear his diary in advance of it. If he could wake tomorrow with little memory of the night before, he would consider it a good night. He rarely drank to excess, but on this occasion felt he deserved to party into oblivion. Let him have this one night when he didn't fall asleep with her face haunting him. Taunting him.

When Jessica grabbed his arm and said Marnie was there, he'd thought she was playing some kind of sick trick on him. He hadn't expected to turn around and actually find her there. In his home. The home she'd walked out of when she'd walked out on him.

A swell of fury rose that she should choose this night of all nights to walk back in. Marnie had forfeited her right to enter his home uninvited, and he had no idea why he hadn't ordered the voidance of her security clearance.

When he reached her, he looked her up and down, well aware that everyone in the basement was watching them, insanely curious as to what she was doing there. 'Hello, sweetheart,' he said, speaking as casually as if the last time he'd seen her she hadn't told him in a voice injected with steel to leave her flat and never come back. 'You should have told me you were coming—I'd have had your cauldron prepared for you.'

She showed no reaction whatsoever to his jibe. 'When I set off, I didn't realise you were having a party.'

'You should have called.'

'I did. I guess you didn't hear your phone over all this noise.'

'It's not noise, it's a party.' He brought his face close to hers. 'A party to celebrate the end of *us*.'

Her plump, heart-shaped lips tightened before she shook her head. 'There was never any *us*, Dom.'

'I'd say that marriage implies a great deal of *us*, but *us* is no more, so I'm afraid it's too late to be regretting your life choices.' He held his hands in the air and wiggled his fingers. 'You're welcome to stay and party. Have a drink or two—who knows, a couple of vodkas inside you might inject you with some personality.'

That jibe hit the mark. Marnie, the woman whose emotions so rarely showed on her face, flinched. The expected satisfaction off the back of it failed to come; instead came an immediate awareness that he'd gone too far.

God damn her. When Carmela, his first wife, left him for his closest friend, he'd been humiliated. That it had come hot on the heels of his elderly father's death had left him devastated, but he hadn't fought the divorce or been cruel in the aftermath. One of the reasons he'd chosen to marry Marnie was that she was too boring for him to develop any great passion for her, and it infuriated him that he'd been unable to stop himself fighting and fighting to force her back to him.

He'd worked closely with her for years, had always found her a very calm and soothing presence in what could be a very combative business, so when he'd turned thirty-five and decided it was time to have the brood of children he'd always wanted while he was still young enough to enjoy them and be around long enough to guide them into adulthood, he'd decided she was the perfect candidate for the role of their mother. Of course, in this day and age, it wasn't necessary for children to go hand in hand with marriage, but Domenico had been raised with the security of parents in a committed marriage and wanted the same for his own offspring.

Not only had Marnie been perfect mother material, she'd been perfect wife material for him too, being too placid and lacking in imagination to even imagine passion. He'd done passion and been burned badly for it, so never again. In all the years he'd known her, Marnie had never questioned him, contradicted him or voiced an opinion to him. She followed his orders to the letter and, most importantly, proved willing to devote her life to his needs. She was perfect! As his wife, she would be content to fit in the background of his life and raise their brood and let him get on with setting the world of corporate law on fire and managing his vast portfolio of investments.

For a year, their marriage had worked pretty much as he'd envisaged it would. The only disappointing aspect was their failure to conceive. Other than that, everything had been great. Marnie had accepted what was required from her without complaint, had never refused his conjugal visits to her bedroom and never bombarded him with demands. And then she'd hit him with those damned divorce papers.

Maybe it would have been easier to accept if he'd seen it coming, but she'd blindsided him. He'd slid the anniversary bracelet across the table to her and gazed at her with avid expectation.

The box had stayed closed. The chameleon eyes which changed colour numerous times a day had filled with sadness, and in that quiet way of hers, she'd said, 'I want a divorce.'

Certain he'd misheard her, he'd tilted his head and grinned. 'Sorry?'

She'd produced an envelope from her bag and handed it to him. 'I saw a solicitor last week and instructed him to start divorce proceedings today. I'm leaving you.'

And that had been that. His docile, compliant wife had walked away from the life of luxury he'd lavished on her and refused to change her mind. Nothing had worked. No cajoling or threats or dirty tricks had been enough to make her see reason, and now he was glad of it. Let her suffer in the bed she'd made for herself. He would find himself another wife to have children with. Not yet, though. Let him blow the cobwebs of celibacy off first and then find wife number three. Third time lucky!

He'd make damned sure that wife number three didn't come with eyes capable of piercing his conscience with nothing but a look. Why the hell was he even feeling guilty over a jibe that was essentially the truth? Marnie had no personality. It wasn't his fault if the truth hurt.

'As scintillating as it is to see you again, I need to get back to my guests. I know the concept of having fun is anathema to you, but for…' But he'd lost his audience for Marnie suddenly covered her mouth with her hand and, without a word, hurried away from him. In a blink, she'd thrown herself into one of the basement's bathrooms.

Marnie barely had time to lock the cubicle door behind her before the vomit came. She only just made it to the toilet in time.

It took a long time to convince herself that it was safe to move her face away. Collapsing onto the cool, tiled floor, she pressed her head back against the wall and prayed for the nausea to abate. She felt awful. The sickness was getting worse. She needed water, but right then she didn't even have the strength to stand up.

God, why hadn't she turned around and gone home as soon as she'd realised he was having a party? He'd have seen her missed calls eventually and called her back.

She heard the main bathroom door open and closed her eyes. There were plenty of bathrooms in the basement, all with a single cubicle entered out of sight of the dance floor. She had to give Domenico his due; he had an eye for detail.

'Marnie?'

She squeezed her eyes even tighter. Oh, what a huge mistake she'd made, coming here like this.

'Are you ill?' The acerbic tone Domenico had taunted her with on the edge of the dance floor was gone. If she didn't know better, she'd think she heard concern in his lightly accented voice.

She swallowed hard. 'I'm fine. Go back to your guests. I'll be out in a minute.'

There was a small pause. 'Are you on the floor?'

'I just need a minute. Please, leave me alone.'

Another pause and then a grim, 'Open the door.'

'Go away, Dom. We'll talk tomorrow.'

'Open the door right now or I'll break it down.'

Close to tears, she choked, 'Go *away*.'

'Last chance. Open it, *now*.'

Marnie knew better than anyone that Domenico never made idle threats. She'd known him since she was eighteen, had worked closely with him for six years and been married to him for one. If he said he'd break the door down, then he'd break the door down, and she couldn't bear that. Any form of violence made her want to hide in her wardrobe and cover her ears like she'd done as a little girl.

It took all her strength to lift her arm and turn the lock.

He swung the door open and gazed down at her.

A wave of misery hit her so hard and so fast that she came within a breath of bursting into tears.

She'd adored this man. Worshipped him. Would have done anything for him.

There was no mockery in the light brown stare. 'You're ill.'

She shook her head and wished again that she'd turned around and gone home. She'd never wanted to tell him like this. In her head, she'd been standing tall, fully in control, ready to take whatever came next, not feeling more vulnerable than she'd ever felt before.

'Not ill,' she whispered. 'Pregnant.'

CHAPTER TWO

THERE WAS A long moment when all Domenico could hear was a loud ringing in his ears.

He stared unblinking at his ex-wife. The long, streaky blond hair chopped in layers framed a pretty heart-shaped face drained of so much colour that the sprinkling of freckles over the pretty nose and high cheekbones were prominent. The chameleon eyes were currently dark blue. She'd lost weight her already slender frame could ill afford to lose.

His heart thumped into life, the memory he'd fought to forget of their last night together suddenly vivid. Their only night together in six months.

It had happened six weeks ago, the day their decree nisi had come through. Right up until that point, he'd still believed she would see sense and come back to him. Fortified by a couple of strong whiskeys, he'd turned up at her tiny flat—*dio*, he hadn't realised until then what a dangerous place she lived in—determined to make one last effort to talk sense into her. She'd been drinking too, he remembered. She'd opened the door with a glass of white wine in her hand, which had surprised him as she didn't drink alcohol. On the tiny coffee table in the tiny living room sat the bottle, over half of it gone.

The little mouse had roared that night. Meek, subservient Marnie had vanished; in her place was a lion who shouted her anger and resentment at Domenico's efforts to make her see reason. Her righteous fury had ignited something in him, not just his own anger and resentment but a hunger that had risen out of nowhere and gripped him, a hunger he'd never wanted, and even now he couldn't remember how their mouths had gone from trading insults and obscenities to trading saliva, but in the blink of an eye they were naked in her bed, making love like it was their last hours on this earth.

It hadn't been their last hours on earth, but it had been their last hours together. In the morning, when he'd woken with a sense of relief that she'd finally be coming back home, she'd turned her back to him and, with a voice of steel, told him to leave.

The euphoria that had come from their unexpected night together had been doused in her coldness, and it was a coldness that had shocked him back to his senses. He'd wanted his wife back, but not like *that*. Never like that.

He'd never wanted any form of passion with her, and so to have shared and experienced all that…

He'd been unable to throw his clothes on quickly enough.

He'd never wanted to see her again.

'Stay there,' he said now, pulling himself together. 'I'll get rid of everyone.'

She gave a weak shake of her head. 'There's no need. It's just morning sickness. Go back to your guests.'

Morning sickness because she was pregnant with the child he'd married her for.

If the situation weren't so serious, he would have laughed at the irony. 'If you think I'm still capable of partying…' He shook his head and dragged air into his lungs. 'Just stay there.'

Alone in the bathroom, Marnie rubbed her mouth to her knees and fought back more tears.

All those months of their marriage spent praying for the baby she'd stupidly convinced herself would magically turn their marriage into the fairy tale she'd dreamed of, and then all those months spent praying for her period while her head and heart fought over what she should do.

His proposal, the day after his thirty-fifth birthday, had set the tone for their marriage, but she'd been too love-blind to see it.

He'd invited her out to lunch, which had immediately alerted her to something being up because Domenico *never* lunched alone with a female employee. He didn't even allow his office door to be closed when alone with a female employee. He was a playboy, but only in his private life, and never put himself in any form of compromising situation with his staff.

At the time, they'd been in Rome, his home city. At the time, Marnie travelled everywhere with him. He'd taken her to a fancy restaurant that mortals needed to book a year in advance to get a table at, but Domenico Cannavaro was no mortal. He was a Roman god.

After thanking her again for his birthday card, he'd added more wine to her untouched glass and stunned her by asking if she wanted children; stunned her because personal matters were never discussed between them. Never. 'Um, sure,' she'd stuttered, her cheeks turning into a flame because in her fantasies, Domenico was the father of her children.

He'd flashed his beautiful teeth. 'So do I. I always thought I would have them by the time I reached thirty-five.'

She'd been unable to think of a response to that.

'I have a proposition for you,' he'd said, unfazed by her silence.

She'd still been too gormless to respond. Her mind had been racing too hard to formulate anything.

'I want children, and you want children, and I believe you would make an excellent mother. What do you say to us marrying?'

If her eyes could have popped out of her head, they would have.

He'd laughed, correctly reading her expression. 'I am being very serious. Trust me, I have given this a great deal of thought, and I can think of no one better suited to bearing my children and raising them with me than you.'

Marnie had carried a thumping great crush on Domenico for six years. From the day she'd met him, he'd been a constant in her mind. She was never late for work, never took a day off sick, and never complained about the overtime because she would never voluntarily miss a minute of his company. The hours spent without him were spent thinking of him, and when she went to bed it was always with the same fantasy of Domenico looking at her and suddenly seeing her as a woman. He would declare his undying love for her and beg her to marry him.

Finally, she'd managed to make her vocal cords work. 'You want to marry me?' she'd stammered, hardly daring to believe her dream was coming true.

'Very much.' He'd lifted his glass. 'What do you say? Will you marry me, Marnie?'

She'd been nodding like a dog in a window before she could get the words out. 'Yes. Yes, of course I'll marry you.'

Suddenly aware the music had stopped playing, the memory faded and Marnie dragged herself onto the small armchair. The queasiness had passed—at least for now—but she felt drained, as if all the life had been sucked out of her.

The door opened. 'The caterers and DJ are still packing up, but all the guests have gone,' Domenico told her quietly. 'Can you walk?'

She nodded and hoped it was the truth.

Upright, she pressed a hand to the wall until the dizziness that came from standing had passed and wished he wouldn't stand so close to her. For years, she'd loved nothing more than inhaling Domenico's scent. Now it hurt her terribly.

'How long have you felt like this?' he asked as she shuffled out of the bathroom and back into the party room that now had the feel of the *Mary Celeste* to it. It was like all the guests had been spirited away without any warning, the only evidence of their existence the glasses and bottles strewn around, many of them still full of alcohol. She dimly wondered what he'd said to get rid of everyone. Whatever excuse he'd made, they would all know it had something to do with her, and she tried not to imagine what the more scurrilous gossips would be saying. Marnie's marriage to Domenico had broken probably a thousand hearts. News of their divorce would have repaired those hearts in super-quick fashion.

'About a week,' she replied as she tried, again, not to allow herself to wonder how many women he'd been with since she'd left him. It had taken superhuman effort not to quiz him about his other women when they'd been married. She'd never had proof he'd been unfaithful; it just seemed a reasonable assumption to make. Marnie was the one who'd spent years fielding calls from disgruntled lovers he'd blocked from his personal phone, and he certainly hadn't married her for love.

'You've known that long?'

'I only took the test this morning.'

He was silent for a moment. 'You waited until the divorce was final before taking it?'

'Yes.' She grabbed the banister of the basement stairs and held it tight. She wouldn't look at him. 'I knew that when it was confirmed I would have to tell you and you'd use it as a weapon to stop the divorce.'

Domenico clenched his jaw at her admission and tempered the surge of fury by the skin of his teeth. 'So you did know.' If Marnie wasn't so obviously unwell, he'd have no compunction in telling her exactly what he thought of her and her deliberate deceit.

Too damned right he'd have tried to stop the divorce being finalised. A baby changed everything.

Her husky voice was tired. 'I didn't know for certain.'

He did some quick mental maths. They'd ripped each other's clothes off six weeks ago. By his reckoning, she must have been carrying this secret for anything between two and four weeks. If he were a gambling man, he'd put his money on her having sat on it for close to four weeks, especially when he worked back to the date of her last period from when they'd still been together. Marnie's menstrual cycle ran like clockwork.

On the ground floor, she flopped onto the nearest armchair in the reception room, too tired to walk to the living area.

'Can I get you a drink?'

Her eyes briefly met his. 'Water, please.'

'Any food?'

A quick shake of her head.

Figuring it would be quicker to get the water himself than ask one of the staff to get it, and needing a moment to get a grip on his growing anger, Domenico went to the kitchen and filled a pint glass for her, oblivious to the caterers clearing up around him.

She took the glass with a murmured thanks and had a few small sips from it.

He sank onto a hard-backed chair close to her and studied her some more. The lighting up here was much brighter than in the basement, and now he could see just how tired she was. And thin. She'd lost more weight than he'd thought in his initial assessment.

'Are you not eating?'

'I try,' she whispered. 'I'm just struggling to hold anything down. I kept trying to put it down to stress, but I think I was in denial.'

'Deliberate denial?' He tried not to sound too pointed.

Her stare fell to the floor. 'Maybe.' He had to strain to hear her, but then her voice strengthened a little as she looked back at him. 'I know this baby is what you married me for, but I'm not coming back to you.'

'We're going to be parents, Marnie.' It was a fight to keep his voice even-tempered. 'You know how I feel about children being raised by committed parents.'

'I do, yes, but I feel just as strongly that children shouldn't be raised by parents who hate each other.'

'I don't hate you.'

Her lips fleetingly curved in a sad smile. 'Since when have you been a liar?'

He ran his fingers through his hair and tried, again, to keep a grip on his temper. The only thing Domenico hated about Marnie was how she'd outmanoeuvred him with the divorce. She'd let him make love to her night after night, never breathing a word about any unhappiness, while behind his back she'd been putting everything in place to leave him. She'd even given the tenants of her flat notice to leave so it would be free on the day she made her move. When she'd left the restaurant after handing him the divorce papers, she'd got into a cab and driven out of his life. He'd returned home and found much of her dressing room empty. While he'd spent his days working, she'd spent hers secretly packing much of her stuff away and transporting it across London. So sneaky had she been that she'd done it all under the household staff's noses, because if they'd been aware of what she was up to, they would have told him immediately.

This was the first time she'd been back in his home since they'd left for their wedding anniversary meal.

Gripping the sides of the armchair, she got unsteadily to her feet. 'We'll have to have the big conversation about our baby's future another time. I need to go home; I don't feel well.'

'*This* is your home.'

Still holding onto the armchair, she speared him with a pained stare. 'This was *never* my home, and even if it was, we're divorced.'

'That was your choice, not mine.'

'Yet you were the one celebrating it with a party. Not me.'

'I wouldn't have celebrated if I'd known you were pregnant.'

'No, you would have been running a rampage through the courts to stop the divorce going through. Never mind what I wanted, it's all about what *you* want. It's always what you want that matters. Everyone else is just a bit player in the production written, directed and starring Domenico Cannavaro.'

'That's not true,' he bit back angrily. 'I gave you everything you could possibly want. I denied you nothing.'

'No, you gave me everything *you* thought I could

possibly want.' Closing her eyes, she shook her head and breathed in through her nose. 'I didn't come here to rake over the past, Dom, and right now I don't have the strength to argue.'

She was the only person he'd never corrected for calling him Dom, he thought dimly as he wondered how the hell he was supposed to play this. Since she'd left him. Marnie had proved herself immune to threats and dirty tricks—she was much, *much* tougher than he'd believed or given her credit for—and impervious to cajoling flattery, but damn it, she was carrying his child. She couldn't expect him to settle for anything less than their remarrying because he was damned if he was going to be a part-time father. He could threaten her with a custody fight, but if he knew Marnie, she'd have already put contingencies in place to stop that happening.

To think he'd admired her clever brain from the day he'd spotted her new face behind the desk of his London reception. She'd mastered the switchboard within a week. Most people needed a month, but Marnie thought like a chess player. When a vacancy had come up on his personal team, he'd thought of the fresh-faced young Englishwoman and her quick, clever brain, and taken a punt on her. Years later, he'd married her thinking he knew her, and it infuriated him to know how badly he'd misjudged her. Domenico prided himself on reading people like books. It was how he outmanoeuvred *them*, was how he'd turned his father's small corporate law firm into the juggernaut it was today.

He would never have imagined she'd turn that clever brain as a weapon on him.

'You look like you're going to be sick again,' he observed, noting the way she was breathing and the fresh loss of colour on her face. She was still to let go of the chair.

She took a few more deep breaths. 'It will pass.' But still she didn't let go.

'How are you planning to get home?'

'Taxi.'

'You're going to sit in the back of a cab filled with other people's body odour for what, thirty minutes?'

Her cheeks puffed out, and then she swallowed before her hand went over her mouth, and she staggered to the bathroom by the front door. Unlike the bathrooms in the basement where the toilets were separated from the handwashing facilities, this was an ordinary bathroom, and when a couple of minutes had passed and he knocked before pushing the unlocked door open, he found her kneeling over the toilet.

He didn't want to feel tenderness for her, but unfortunately he was human, and so it was impossible not to feel it for someone so clearly suffering. Crouching beside her, he gently rubbed her back. From the contents of the bowl, there had been nothing in her stomach to vomit up.

It was when she let him help her to her feet that he understood what a bad state she was really in, and even as he wondered how the hell she'd made it across London to him, he was working out how he could play it to his advantage.

'Listen to me,' he said once he'd helped her out of the bathroom and back to the armchair. 'You're in no fit state to be travelling anywhere. Stay here for the night.'

Her chin wobbled, and she shook her head.

'I know staying here is the last thing you want, but you're not well, Marnie. How are you going to manage the stairs to your flat?' She lived on the eighth floor of a tower block that would look at home in a dystopian movie. That one time Domenico had visited her there, the elevators had been out of order. The stench of the stairwells had been strong enough to make his eyes water, so God knew what the elevators would smell like when they were working.

Her little flat had been a clean, bright, fresh oasis of tranquillity amidst a sea of detritus.

A tear rolled down her cheek.

He looked away. He'd never seen her cry before and didn't particularly care to see it now. Especially didn't care for the tightening in his chest from it.

'How about we make a deal? You stay here for the night, and in the morning, if you're feeling well enough to travel, I'll get one of the drivers to take you home.'

A long time passed before she sniffed and wiped the tear away with her fingers. 'You promise you'll take me home in the morning?' she whispered.

He scented victory. 'I promise. Let's get you upstairs to bed,' he added before she could change her mind.

But victory was indeed his as all the fight had gone out of her. Docile as a newborn lamb, she let him wrap an arm around her and leaned her weight into him so he could help her back to her feet. No sooner was she upright than she was swaying, fisting his shirt in an effort to hold herself steady.

The ground floor of Domenico's London home had triple-high ceilings, which meant triple the number of stairs to climb to reach the first floor. Marnie was in no fit state to climb them. She must have known it too, for when he lifted her into his arms, she looped her arms around his neck without protest.

Domenico was six foot three, Marnie a good foot shorter than him and probably half his weight, but she felt much lighter in his arms than he'd imagined she would. More fragile, too. As he carefully made his way up the cantilevered stairs, her hair tickled his throat and chin and he kept catching wafts of her shampoo. It was a familiar scent that filled his chest with a pang of emotion so sharp he assumed it came from knowing she was, finally, carrying his child. For that alone, he would take care of her during this sickness and work at forgiving her blatant treachery over the timing of telling him.

She couldn't seriously believe a piece of paper dissolving their marriage meant they wouldn't get back together. It was obvious that pregnancy hormones had conspired to convince her of the rightness of the path she'd taken in leaving him when all she had to do was open the door of her flat to realise what a foolish mistake she'd made. Marnie had to know it would be much better for their child to live with both its parents as a family under the shelter of Domenico's enormous wealth.

Yes, he decided, his plan formulating quickly. He

would work hard to rid himself of his fury at all her underhanded behaviour these last six months, and if he could make that effort, then she could work to rid herself of her anger at his supposed failings as a husband. Hadn't they worked in complete harmony for six years without a cross word between them?

With a little coaxing, she would soon come to her senses. Now that she had a child to think of, she would accept that it was in everyone's best interest for them to remarry.

Only when he opened his bedroom door did she come back to life with a quiet, 'No.'

'I need to be able to watch over you,' he pointed out reasonably, keen to start being all solicitous and caring over her condition.

'No. My room.'

As he'd talked himself into a forgiving and giving mood, he acquiesced without further argument and opened the door to the adjacent room. Gently, he deposited her on the bed. 'I'll get you some water. Do you need anything else?'

She shook her head.

'Do you want to borrow a T-shirt to sleep in?' He'd kept everything she'd left behind in her dressing room until exactly five weeks and six days ago, when he'd returned to his home from his night in her flat and ordered everything to be donated to charity. To think he'd been a breath away from ordering it all to be doused in petrol and set alight! If Marnie had learned about that, he imagined she might take it personally, so it was just as well he'd decided she wasn't worth the cost of the petrol.

The next shake of her head was more violent.

Promising to return shortly with fresh water, Domenico slipped out of the room and finally allowed himself a smile of grim satisfaction that his not-so-docile Marnie was back where she belonged and, even better, was pregnant with the child they'd both so longed for.

CHAPTER THREE

MARNIE WOKE TO dusky morning light with a head aching as badly the nausea crippling her stomach and as badly as the misery gripping the rest of her. She didn't even have to think to know where she was. She was back in her old room. Domenico would be sleeping on the other side of the dividing wall.

Lifting her aching head, she reached for the glass of water she had no recollection of him bringing to her. Her last memory was of kicking off her sandals and crawling beneath the duvet. Beside the glass was a box of tissues and a packet of ginger biscuits, and her heart clenched sharply to know he must have sent someone out to buy them for her.

She drank the water slowly, knowing from experience that drinking too quickly only agitated the nausea. A bucket had been left at the foot of the bed by her head.

When she'd drunk half the water, she put her aching head back on the pillow and prayed to feel better soon. It had been twenty hours since she'd forced a slice of toast down. Her stomach was empty, she needed to eat, but she couldn't face nibbling even one biscuit.

She needed to start feeling better soon, not just for her baby's sake—it needed much more nutrition than Marnie was currently able to provide—but for her own. She'd never imagined morning sickness could feel this bad. The way she currently felt, she didn't feel strong enough to walk to the bathroom, never mind cross London to her flat.

At least the room was cool. Temperatures in London had been roasting in recent weeks, and her flat didn't have air conditioning. It was the only positive she could cling to, especially when she heard the faint sound of Domenico's shower running, and it increased her misery to realise how attuned she still was to all the old noises of her old life. The old noises of Domenico waking and coming to life.

She supposed he would check on her when he was dressed; imagined he was this moment dreaming up some new Machiavellian scheme to make her remarry him. Running one of the world's most successful corporate law firms had made him an expert in the art of playing dirty, and he'd used his full armoury on her.

She could only assume his carrying her into his bedroom had been another of those dirty ploys. She'd never crossed its threshold before. She'd never been invited. She'd never been carried in his arms, not even on their wedding night.

She wished she'd asked him to take her to one of the guest rooms. There were no memories of her old life in the other rooms. All her best memories had been made in this room. All her worst memories since childhood too. They were one and the same, and when she closed her eyes, the best and worst of those memories swam before her. Their wedding night.

Everything had happened super-quickly, only four weeks between proposal and wedding. Domenico had taken charge of everything. He'd been the one to decide they would marry in an English registry office with only his mother, sister, brother-in-law and two small nephews as their guests. His reasoning had been that he'd already had a big white wedding in Italy. It hadn't occurred to him that Marnie might have wanted to marry in a church, and he'd displayed zero curiosity when she'd turned down his oh-so-gracious offer of inviting her closest family too. Domenico had been the one to decide that their celebratory meal with their handful of guests should be in a pretty countryside hotel and that they would return to London in the evening for a huge celebratory party. That party had been held in the basement of this very house. The guest list had run into the hundreds. He'd shown zero curiosity at Marnie's failure to add any names of her own to it.

Instead of being upset at his taking charge and organising the wedding entirely for his wants and needs and his complete lack of curiosity about her, Marnie had been too busy floating on her cloud of dreams to remove the blinkers from her eyes. She was marrying Domenico! All her dreams were coming true!

She'd been pathetic.

Once the guests had gone, he'd led her upstairs—without taking her hand—and opened the door to this room. Finally, she'd thought, Domenico would express his inner feelings for her. The fact he'd held off making love, held off even kissing her, was proof of how meaningful this, their first night together, was. She'd had so much excitement charging through her veins that she'd had to imagine her feet had glue on the soles to stop herself from bouncing.

When she looked back on the Marnie who'd climbed into this bed with such high hopes and fairy-tale dreams, she wanted to rip the blinkers off and shout some sense into her.

Instead of carrying her over the threshold, he'd told her he was going to take a quick shower and to make herself comfortable, then left the room, which had killed her fantasy of him carrying her to the bed and laying her down on it. Her cloud of dreams, though, had been very resilient, and she'd showered in the pretty, feminine bathroom thinking he must be wanting to build the anticipation. Her blinkers had remained when she brushed her teeth with the only toothbrush in the pot, stayed firmly on when she slipped the white silk negligee she'd splurged half her salary on as a surprise for him, and continued to blind her when she gazed around the beautiful bedroom that was as feminine as the bathroom and practically the same size as her flat. She would swear the bed was bigger than her entire kitchen.

Innate shyness had gripped her when Domenico finally joined her in the bedroom. She was waiting for him in bed, and smiled timidly at his wide grin as he strode across the room wearing nothing but a pair of snug black hipster boxers which he'd nonchalantly shucked down his muscular legs and stepped out of, as blasé about his nudity as she was shy about hers. And why should he not be blasé? His body was as beautiful as the rest of him, and her already pounding heart came close to punching through her ribs that first time she saw him in all his naked glory. He was perfect. Everything about him, from the muscular leanness of his physique to the deep olive hue of his skin, to the dark hair that neatly covered his chest. Even the huge appendage between his legs was beautiful…not that she had anything to compare it to.

He'd climbed onto the bed, and then he'd climbed on top of her.

'Had a good day?' he asked when his face was over hers, his tone the same as all the times he'd asked her on a Monday morning if she'd had a good weekend.

Her senses engulfed, full to bursting with emotion, she'd nodded, pleading with her eyes for him to kiss her.

This was it. The fulfilment of all her dreams.

When she'd felt the first brush of his lips on hers, she'd melted, melted so deeply that it took a long while for the thought to hover in her near-delirious mind that his expert kisses and caresses were *too* expert. Domenico was going through all the motions she'd read about and seen in films; preparing her for sex—and preparing her beautifully, every touch and every kiss heavenly—but there was something missing and she'd had the fleeting thought that she was being made love to by an android plugged into *expert lover* mode. The only real hint of human emotion had come when he'd deemed her ready and rubbed the head of that huge appendage between her legs, and she'd whispered, 'You will be careful?'

For the first time since their first kiss, he'd looked in her eyes, a slight frown in his brow. 'You've not done this before?'

She'd shaken her head.

His lips had tightened, jaw clenching, and there had been a beat of a moment when she'd been certain he was going to climb off her. But it had only lasted a beat. His features had relaxed into their normal gorgeous, amiable state. 'Just relax. I'll take care of you.'

He'd been as good as his word. He'd eased himself inside her slowly, and she'd been so turned on that she'd experienced only the slightest discomfort. It had felt good. Really good. But even as he'd brought her to her first ever orgasm, there had been a disconnect in her head, like she was hovering on the ceiling watching herself climax and trying to pinpoint what was missing.

When it was over, she'd lain beneath him with her heart pounding and the feel of his heart thumping between their meshed bodies, and found herself faintly surprised that there was a beating heart in him.

He'd eased himself off her and rolled onto his back.

They'd both gazed at the ceiling, neither talking.

The silence had been deafening.

Goose bumps had broken out on her flesh, but she'd been too shy to pull the duvet up, a horrible feeling stealing over her that now he'd spent himself, she'd become invisible to him and he wouldn't be happy at the reminder that she lay there beside him.

He'd sat up and run his fingers through his hair. The

muscles of his back had moved with the motion. Her throat had closed, the ache to trace her hands over his smooth skin unbearable as it came with an instinctive fear that her touch wouldn't be welcome.

The familiar smile had been on his face when he turned his head slightly to look at her. 'I should leave you to get some sleep. A member of the housekeeping team is always on call, so just press the intercom if you need anything.'

Even now, she could remember her eyes widening in shock, but her tongue tying in retreat.

He'd leaned over to place a fleeting, dutiful kiss on her mouth. 'Sleep well, Marnie.'

He'd pulled his boxers back on and strolled out of the room without looking back at her. She hadn't uttered a single word of protest. She'd been incapable. Marnie had learned at a very young age that in times of conflict, silent invisibility was the safest course of action. More often than not, it hadn't been necessary to make herself invisible because that's what she'd already been to her parents, but lessons learned in childhood were the ones that stuck in your psyche the deepest.

Until their wedding night, Marnie had never felt invisible to Domenico.

Looking back, it wasn't conflict that she'd been frightened of with him that night—he wasn't the kind of man to raise a hand to a woman, he just wasn't—but that to question him would lead to answers she wasn't ready to hear. The fairy tale she'd built her dreams on was tumbling around her, and one wrong word would see it crumble into dust.

Nausea grabbed her, the water she'd drunk determined to expel itself out of her. She was leaning with her head out of the bed, vomiting clear fluid into the bucket when Domenico came into the room.

Without saying a word, he sat beside her and gently gathered her hair away from her face. When the retches had subsided and she'd wiped her mouth with one of the tissues and pulled her aching head back onto the pillow, she didn't have the strength to protest when he stretched out beside her and tenderly spooned her to him, careful not to put any pressure on her stomach.

She didn't have the strength, either, to lie to herself that his silent support wasn't comforting. That being here with him and being taken care of like this wasn't comforting.

'I think it's time we called a doctor out, don't you?' he said quietly. His breath was warm against the back of her head.

A tear rolled down her cheek, and suddenly she was terrified. The severity of her morning sickness *wasn't* normal, and it was a sickness that was accelerating.

'Marnie?'

Squeezing her eyes shut as if it could drive away her terror that their baby was in danger, she nodded.

He kissed her hair, then moved away and climbed off the bed to make the calls that would no doubt have one of London's top obstetricians there within the hour.

Domenico breathed deeply before opening the door.

To his huge relief, Marnie was sitting up in her hospital bed. The IV to replenish all her lost fluids that she'd been hooked back onto when he'd left the hospital for the night had been removed. She'd even regained a little colour in her cheeks.

She gave a fleeting smile at his appearance.

He moved the guest chair closer to the bed. 'How are you feeling?' he asked as he sat.

Another fleeting smile. 'Better.'

'The anti-sickness is working now?'

'So far. They gave me the new one when I woke up, and the toast I ate has stayed down.'

Hyperemesis gravidarum. It sounded like a spell in a book about witches and wizards, but no, it was the technical name for severe morning sickness. Marnie hadn't wanted to take the anti-sickness drugs, had only submitted when the doctor assured her it wouldn't harm the baby.

That had been the moment Domenico realised she already loved their baby. Whether her denial about the pregnancy had been deliberate or not, the baby was already a part of her.

'That's great news.' She'd vomited up the first anti-sickness drug while the second one, administered by injection, had had little effect, so it was another huge relief to know the third one they'd tried was working. There had been talk about tube feeding her to bypass her stomach, just to get some nutrients into her.

The consultant came into the room and greeted them with his usual professional smile. 'I hear you're finally on the mend,' he said to Marnie.

She looked at the consultant as if he were a deity come to life. 'It doesn't feel like I'm dying now.'

'We do our best,' he said wryly. 'I've looked at your charts and want to keep an eye on you for a while longer, but if your blood pressure remains stable and you keep holding food down, then there is no reason we can't discharge you later this afternoon…with caveats, of course.'

Her blond eyebrows drew together in question.

He perched himself on the bottom of her bed. 'Don't let yourself be fooled into believing this is over for you. Even with the antiemetics, you're still going to feel nauseous and need plenty of rest.'

'How long will I feel like this?'

'At the least until you're through the first trimester, but it's different for all women. We're going to be keeping a very close eye on you and the baby for the rest of the pregnancy, so however long it lasts for you, we will be on hand to help manage it.'

'Thank you.' Her smile was softer than any smile she'd given Domenico. 'That's reassuring to hear.'

'Before we discharge you, I'll get one of the team to speak to you about how best to manage your symptoms at home.' He turned to Domenico. 'You'll need to be there for that talk—I'm entrusting your wife into your care.'

'Ex-wife,' Marnie interjected before Domenico could agree. 'We're divorced.'

The consultant made an owl-like blink. 'My apologies. I wasn't aware. Your file hasn't been updated.'

'The divorce was only finalised four days ago.'

'Right…' He was clearly flummoxed at the news, which was understandable seeing as Marnie had been an inpatient for three days and Domenico had been a constant by her side and was footing all the bills.

'I'm the baby's father,' Domenico felt compelled to confirm, and ignored the bitterness this confirmation provoked. If Marnie hadn't been so desperate to divorce him, she'd have taken the pregnancy test much sooner. He'd have found a way to stop the divorce from being finalised, and there would be no question about his paternity. 'And I'm more than willing to have Marnie discharged into my care.'

'Good, good.' The consultant nodded vigorously, acting like it was an everyday occurrence to have a patient pregnant by her ex-husband, then cleared his throat and looked at Marnie. 'Are you happy to be discharged into your ex-husband's care?'

She shook her head. 'No. I want to go home. To *my* home.'

'You have someone there who can take care of you?'

A slower shake of her head.

'Do you have a parent or sibling you can stay with until you're well enough to take care of yourself? A close friend? I can make the call for you.'

Eyes clouding, her chin wobbled, but her voice was strong. 'I've been taking care of myself for a long time.'

The consultant's pager beeped. He read its message and rose. 'I'm needed with another patient.' He fixed his stare back on Marnie. 'Think about what you want to do. I'm sure we can come up with a solution, but I do not feel at all comfortable discharging you to an empty home.'

If Domenico wasn't watching her so carefully, he'd have missed the wary glance Marnie shot at him.

For three days, she'd been too ill to display any animosity to Domenico. In fact, he'd had the distinct impression she was grateful; glad even, that he'd spent his days in the hospital with her, his vigil continuing even after they'd been assured the baby wasn't in any danger. At the very least, she hadn't told him to leave. Now she was feeling better, he sensed the stubbornness that had been her trademark these last six months reassert itself.

'I'm not letting you go back to that flat,' he told her firmly as soon as the consultant had closed the door.

Her stare was tired but baleful. 'You don't get a say in it.'

'I do. That's my baby you're carrying.'

'Yes, but I'm the one responsible for bringing it safely into the world.'

'And I'm responsible for keeping you well enough to bring it safely into the world.'

'You're not my husband. You have no responsibility for me.'

'I might not be your husband anymore, but we are equally responsible for the pregnancy, and I am not having the mother of my child living alone in that shithole when she's ill and in need of care.'

She shot him a look of pure venom. 'My home is *not* a shithole.'

'How are you going to manage if you go back there?' he demanded, ignoring her refutation. 'Who are you going to turn to when you need help? The drug dealers in the apartment next door?'

'They're not drug dealers.'

'No, I'm sure they're upstanding citizens who just happen to be cultivating their own cannabis farm. They don't even try to disguise the smell. And have your landlords bothered to fix the elevators or are you going to drag your depleted body up eight flights of stairs to reach your apartment?' Her jaw clenched, proving he'd hit the mark with that one, and he continued pressing his point. 'And what about food? How are you going to nourish yourself the times you can't get out of bed, and let's consider, too, the nursing staff tasked with home visits to you—how do you think they'll feel making visits to a neighbourhood where they'll be lucky not to have the tyres of their cars stolen?'

Anger slashed her cheeks. 'What gives you the right to be so judgmental?' she said tremulously. 'That's my *home* you're talking about.'

'Stating facts is not making judgments. Your condition is serious, Marnie, and you're approaching the point where it's going to get worse before it gets better.'

Marnie turned her face away and closed her eyes. There was no point asking if he'd researched her condition. Domenico researched everything. When he took on a new client, he would research them to the nth degree along with every aspect of their case from every angle and permutation. Everything he researched, he retained in the file he kept in his brain. No other lawyer was better prepared, able to pluck seemingly fatuous knowledge from nowhere and able to think more quickly on his feet. It was one of the reasons he was so wildly successful in his chosen career that governments begged him to represent them, and this thirst for knowledge wasn't restricted to the law. Domenico was curious about everything, and she had no doubt he was now as knowledgeable as the consultant about her condition. If he said it was going to get worse before it got better, then she believed him.

'If you come home with me, you'll be looked after twenty-four-seven,' he said into the silence. 'You know this.'

She did know it. Dom's household staff were good people. She'd known most of them for years, from her time as his PA when she'd been on the same staff divide as them.

She knew his suggestion made perfect sense. She knew she would struggle to take care of herself the way she currently felt. On a list of pros and cons, there would be a good fifty pros for moving back in with Domenico for a while and only one con. But that one con was a massive con. It meant being back under Domenico's roof.

And then he uttered the killer line that made her accept defeat. 'You know this is the best thing all round, for you *and* for the baby.'

Swallowing hard, she turned her face back to him. 'If I come home with you, it's on the strict proviso that it's only until I feel better.'

She caught the flash of triumph in his eyes. 'If that's what you want.'

'It is.'

'But I have a proviso of my own, which is that you reserve the right to change your mind whenever you please and stay forever.'

'That's my second proviso.'

He leaned his face a little closer. 'That you'll stay forever?'

'No, that you accept it's only a temporary situation and that I'm not coming back to you. I want you to promise you won't even mention making it permanent or us remarrying.'

'I can agree to that.'

'Promise me. No talk of any kind of a future where you and I get back together. Promise it or I go back to my flat.'

He sighed and shook his head with the air of a man making an indulgent concession. 'I promise.'

CHAPTER FOUR

THE ELEVATORS IN Marnie's tower block were working. However, the stench that wafted out of the nearest when the door slid open was so revolting that Domenico gagged and opted to climb the eight flights of stairs.

Why the hell would any sane person choose to live somewhere like this, he wondered as he neared a group of young adolescents openly smoking cannabis at the top of the seventh flight. They barely looked old enough to have pimples, never mind the bullish swagger they all adopted at his approach.

He gave a nod of acknowledgement as he passed and wondered how much of the stench in this place they'd contributed towards. Then he wondered where the hell their parents were.

Aware of their stares following him and the rude catcalls being aimed at him, he didn't break stride as he continued up the final flight, rightly judging they were more intimidated of him than they wanted him to be of them, and not for the first time wondered why the hell Marnie had chosen to live in a dangerous shithole like this. He got that it was cheap, but, hell, surely there were safer cheap places a young woman would choose to live in the capital? Whatever her reasons, he was damned if his child would ever set foot within two hundred metres of it. He'd sooner raze it to the ground than let that happen.

Using the key she'd given him, he let himself into Marnie's flat. It was like entering an oven. Even so, he took a welcome breath of the clean, albeit baking, air inside it.

Despite its godawful location, there was something very soothing about the interior. The walls in the small living/dining room were plain white, the furniture generic simplicity at its best, but it was in all the soft furnishing and accents that she'd made her quiet mark with soothing pastel shades for the cushions and curtains and an abundance of framed photos, books and scented candles neatly crammed on the plentiful shelves of the living room walls.

The tiny kitchen, he guessed from its style, had last been modernised before Marnie was born, but she'd made her peaceful mark in there too. All the cupboard doors had been painted a soft, dusky pink, the worktops overlaid with a fake white marble surface. Everything was immaculate.

Unable to resist his one chance to observe her in the wild, so to speak, he opened the cupboards and found a surprising variety of tins and jars and packets and baking ingredients, and an equally surprising array of gadgets, the kind of gadgets only people who loved to cook bought. Neatly stacked on the top of a cupboard were flatpack silver boxes, and he suddenly thought of the cakes she used to bring in if they were in London when a member of the team celebrated a birthday. Domenico had been born without a sweet tooth, but even he'd been unable to resist those moreish treats she always presented in a silver box. He'd assumed she bought them at a bakery on her way to the office, remembered once, years back, telling her to give him the bill so he could reimburse her and Marnie shrugging it off with a smile and saying it was her pleasure to do it. He'd never guessed she made them herself, was certain she'd never told anyone she baked the cakes they all devoured like locusts.

His throat feeling weirdly tight, he looked in the fridge. It was stocked with an abundance of fruit and vegetables that would never be eaten. On the kitchen windowsill sat two cherry tomato plants, ripe with fruit, but their stems withered from not being watered in four days. After filling a plastic box he found with the bounty of the tomatoes Marnie had lovingly grown and cared for, he finally set off to do the job she'd entrusted him with.

He hesitated at the bedroom's threshold, memories suddenly assailing him.

This was the room they'd conceived their child in.

He'd already been inside her when they'd stumbled over this threshold. Marnie's limbs had been wrapped tight around him. In front of him was the bed they'd fallen onto, still ripping each other's clothes off as they fucked like a dam whose walls had been breached, their coupling the water pouring in a torrent to flood everything in its path.

He'd never had an experience like it. Not just the

sex itself but the feelings that had gone with it, the urgency, the need, the hunger. The desperation. It had all been there in one hedonistic night of madness. And it had been in both of them. Marnie hadn't been the passive bed partner of their marriage. On the bed in front of him, she'd cradled his head while he'd suckled her breasts and she'd ridden up and down his length.

By the time they'd made love a third time, it would have taken a crane to remove him from the bed. Even if he'd been capable of leaving, the drugged-like need for her had remained alive in his veins. For the first time since they'd married, he'd fallen asleep with Marnie in his arms.

They'd held each other all night long, and then, in the morning, long after the sun had come up, she'd opened her eyes only a beat after he'd opened his.

For a singular moment in time, a connection the like of which he'd never known could exist had flown between them, a connection so powerful that something that had felt close to euphoria had caught hold of him, and he'd smiled from the rush of it all and bowed his head to kiss her.

Their mouths never made contact. In barely a blink, that singular connection between them was severed. Marnie's beautiful face tightened, almost crumbling before she pulled herself out of his arms and rolled away from. With her back to him, she'd quietly told him to leave.

Only now, back in the room where it had all happened, could he not deny how those words had gut-punched him.

Rejection after a night like that wouldn't sit well with anyone, but that had felt…

He closed his eyes and breathed out slowly.

In the moments of Marnie's rejection, he'd felt more sucker-punched than when Carmela had told him she was leaving him for Davide.

He sat on the bed and expelled another long breath.

He'd been careful to ensure his marriage to Marnie was nothing like his marriage to Carmela; had been clear from the outset that it was primarily the mother of his child he'd been seeking in a wife. He hadn't wanted a wife as a lover in the traditional sense because that's when emotions reared, and he would never allow himself to be entangled with emotions again. He'd been ready for the children he'd always wanted and so needed to marry so his children could have the same love and stability that he'd been fortunate to have, but if he was going to commit to marriage again, he needed to be sure it would be for life.

Domenico had learned the hard way that passion could not be trusted. When passion burned itself out, bitterness rose and marriages fell.

He'd planned it all perfectly. His docile, placid Marnie, his most loyal and conscientious worker, would be perfectly content to fall in line with his plans. He would share her bed to create the child they both wanted, but they would spend their lives as companions rather than lovers, much as his parents' successful marriage had worked. If Domenico wanted hot sex, he would look elsewhere—Marnie wouldn't mind at all—but to create a successful marriage, it needed to be as companions. Any love that grew would be a platonic love. Unlike passionate love, platonic love was stable and reliable. Trustable.

The only doubt he'd experienced throughout the whole thing was when she'd shyly confirmed her virginity. An emotion he still didn't understand had gripped him, and he'd had a sudden flash of the way she often blushed when he caught her staring at him. His heart had sunk.

It had been because of her virginity and those blushes that he'd left her bed as soon as was decent once the deed was done. He'd known it was imperative to reinforce the parameters of their marriage immediately, for Marnie's sake. Obviously, he hadn't thought for a moment that she could be in love with him—he hadn't believed she had the imagination to fall in love… or, at least that's what he'd told himself—but at the time, it had felt very necessary, a means of protecting her from herself if she needed it. You didn't have to love someone to care for them, and he'd cared for her, and he'd gone out of his way to ensure their marriage was a good one for her. He'd given her a generous—very generous—allowance along with an unlimited credit card and the use of any car in his fleet that she so wished to use. He'd lavished her with jewellery and mini-breaks, taken her on regular date nights, called her every evening when he was abroad on business and always brought her gifts back from them. When he'd joined her in her bed, sex had been—necessarily so—straightforward and perfunctory, but he'd been a considerate lover and had always made sure to bring her to orgasm before taking his own release.

Strangely, despite his pre-marriage imaginings and his certainty that Marnie wouldn't care, he'd never been tempted to seek hot sex elsewhere, so he'd been faithful too. Not one woman had caught his eye.

She'd walked away from it all without looking back. He was only here in her flat now because she'd wanted to collect some clothes when she was discharged. He'd resisted saying it would be over his dead body before she came back to this shithole. Instead, he'd offered to collect whatever she needed to save her fragile body from traipsing to the other side of London and back. He was quite sure she'd agreed only because she knew how much he loathed the place. And also because she'd seen the sense in what he was saying. He'd known better than to offer to buy her a new wardrobe of clothes, especially as this had come on the heels of his promise not to discuss their future together. She hadn't needed to see him cross his fingers to know his promise had been a false one and that he was simply biding his time…

A framed photo on one of her bedroom shelves suddenly caught his eye and cut through his train of thought. He pulled it down and studied it closely. It was a picture of Marnie as a child, maybe aged five or six, with her cheek pressed against a woman who looked so much like her she had to be Marnie's mother. Or maybe her grandmother. Her age was hard to determine. Both subjects were smiling, but it was the window behind them that had really caught his attention, and he carried it to the living room and held it in front of the window there, slowly moving backwards as he compared what was in the photo with what lay before him.

His heart lurched.

The windows were the same. The photo had been taken in this room.

Domenico's prediction that Marnie's sickness would get worse before it got better proved prophetic. Despite the anti-sickness medication and all the other things she'd been prescribed, it wasn't until the fifteen-week mark of the pregnancy that she began to hope she was turning a corner. It was catching the scent of lamb cooking and her stomach barely twitching in reaction that gave her that hope. Strong scents had been as triggering as strong tastes. For close to three months she'd survived on the blandest foods imaginable, topped up with nutritious supplements specifically designed to be tasteless.

After weeks and weeks and weeks of exhaustion, she now, at sixteen weeks, was regaining her energy too, and had spent much of the day looking forlornly out of her bedroom window at the rain lashing down on Domenico's gorgeous garden. She wished she could be out in it. Summer had stretched into autumn without her even noticing.

If she hadn't kept such a firm hold on how far along she was with the pregnancy—she'd been surprised to learn the due date being taken by the date of her last period meant she was further along than she'd assumed—she'd have lost track of how long she'd been back here under Domenico's roof. Eight weeks. She'd never imagined when she agreed to stay with him that it would stretch so long. The twelve-week pregnancy mark had come and gone with unspoken relief from them both that the baby had survived that far.

There had been much left unspoken between them since her temporary return, the future being the biggest unspoken 'thing.' Domenico's work schedule was as manic as it always was, but he'd reduced his social life to nothing. He left her medical care to the experts, but in the evenings that he was home, he plonked himself in her room. He intuitively knew if she was having a good or bad day. If she was having a bad one, he quietly got on with checking his investments and seeing if he'd had another billion added to his net worth since his last check. When Marnie had first realised the extent of his vast wealth, she'd wondered why on earth he continued running his law firm. She'd soon come to see that he thrived on all that came with it, not just the pressure, but that when practising law, there was always a clear-cut winner and loser.

Domenico thrived on winning, and it was this competitive aspect of his nature that kept her guard high, especially when she'd had a reasonably good day and he spent the evenings good-humouredly regaling her with tales from the office or giving a running commentary on whatever sport he happened to be watching on her TV.

Marnie had beaten him in their divorce, a loss that was anathema to him, and as far as he was concerned, her waiting for their divorce to be finalised to take the pregnancy test was on a par with cheating.

To Domenico's mind, the pregnancy meant the game had been reset. He was simply biding his time. When he judged the time to be right, he would restart the game. She knew it, and he knew she knew it. What she didn't know was how far he was prepared to go to win, not now that the stakes were so high.

Currently, he was flying back from Washington, where he'd spent five days overseeing the lobbying of the federal government for one of the firms he represented. Once upon a time, Marnie would have been all over the details of it, and it still saddened her to remember how he used to joke that she knew more about his clients and corporate law than he did. He'd never realised she had zero personal interest in his branch of law and that she'd soaked in all the details for him, not to impress him, but to make life easier for him and save him time. If he needed a fact or figure on a case or client, she could produce it in an instant, and she'd been devastated when she'd realised marrying him meant she would no longer be working for him.

'You don't need to work now,' he'd said with his easy charm two days after their wedding when she'd joined him for breakfast dressed for the office. There had been no time for a honeymoon for the newlyweds.

Their first full day as a married couple had been spent, at Domenico's insistence, making a dent in the credit card he'd presented her with, shopping for a wardrobe fit for Domenico Cannavaro's wife. He'd come along with her, given much constructive feedback on the selected items without showing a hint of boredom, and even taken her for lunch at one of London's most exclusive hotels. If she'd had a brother, she imagined that's what going shopping with him would have been like. Fun, but with zero physical affection or intimacy.

'But I love my job,' she'd protested that second morning, taken aback as he'd never given a hint that he wanted her to stop working for him.

He'd smiled indulgently. 'I know, but when you get pregnant, I'm going to need to find a replacement for you, so it makes sense to start as we mean to go on. Being my wife and the mother of my children is your job now, Marnie, and I know you're going to be as great at it as you were at being my assistant.'

In the blink of an eye, she'd gone from spending regular ten-hour days with him and seeing much of the world by his side to being the little wife at home.

Had she stood up for herself and insisted on continuing with her job until their first baby came along? Of course she hadn't. She'd fallen into line because that's what she always did, and when he'd left for the office without her, she'd given herself a good talking to and vowed to be the best wife it was possible to be, just as he expected.

What she should have done was pack her bags and leave him, but her love blinkers hadn't fallen off at that point, only become a little smudged.

The irony that her love blinkers finally fell off around the time Domenico, increasingly desperate for her to conceive, cut down on his international travel and joined her in her bed every night he was in London was one she would have laughed at if she hadn't come to hate him.

There hadn't been any big drama over the loss of her blinkers. In all their marriage, they'd never exchanged one cross word. No, it was more that the blinkers had become so smudged that eventually they'd fallen off under the sheer weight of grime stuck to them, and suddenly she'd seen herself as he'd seen her: as his chattel, a walking, talking, Domenico-pleasing doll, invisible to the eye unless needed for playing with, and devoid of life and needs of her own.

He didn't want her any more than her parents had. He only wanted what he'd pigeon-holed her into being for him.

By the time she'd left him, Marnie had been resentful of every orgasm he'd brought her to.

She'd never understood why she'd missed him so badly. And she didn't understand why she missed his presence so badly now.

Domenico swept through his front door, rubbing the rain from his hair as he exchanged a friendly greeting with Clive, his butler, and was updated on pertinent household news. About to climb the stairs to see Marnie, Clive cleared his throat and said, 'Ms Ware is in the orangery.'

If there was one thing Domenico hated, it was his very English butler's new way of referring to Marnie, and if there was one thing he hated more, it was that he couldn't correct him as she wasn't his wife anymore and had dropped his surname when she'd filed the divorce papers.

Biting back the burst of piqued fury, he nodded his thanks and headed off.

The orangery was a sprawling conservatory-type room that wrapped around the east wing of the house. It was a room he rarely visited; had only refrained from turning it into an indoor tennis court because his mother liked to pretend she was English gentry when she visited and take afternoon tea in it. His mother didn't even like tea.

Stepping into it, he saw the change in Marnie with one glance. She was curled on a rattan sofa at the far end, reading. Her long, choppily layered blond hair was loose and looked recently brushed, the clothing he could see that wasn't hidden by the blanket on her lap looked like daywear rather than the oversized pyjamas she'd spent eight weeks living in. Although his staff had provided regular updates in his absence, seeing the marked improvement for himself released such unadulterated relief that he sank onto the footstool by her feet with a beaming grin.

For all the complicated contradictions of Domenico's feelings for Marnie, there had been nothing complicated about how he'd felt watching her suffer these last few months. He'd hated it. If he could have infused her suffering into his own body and set hers free, he would have done.

'You look *well*.' A week ago, she'd said she thought the nausea was easing. Now, for the first time in eight weeks, she had a touch of colour in her cheeks. Her eyes—he couldn't decide if they looked grey or blue today—were brighter than they'd looked in eight weeks, too, the bruises of exhaustion that had lived beneath them much faded.

The touch of a smile curved her cheeks. 'I'm feeling stronger every day. If I carry on like this, I should be able to go home soon.'

That was definitely a hint of challenge in her voice. She really was improving!

Refusing to take the bait, he instead turned it to his advantage. 'Let's get you to full strength before we discuss that step, and I have just the thing to get you there.'

She arched an eyebrow in perfect suspicion.

'Let's go to Rome. They're predicting another two weeks of rain here, but in Rome, they're forecasting sunshine.' And he knew Marnie loved his Roman villa. It was the perfect place and setting for her recovery. The romantic nature of the place meant it fit perfectly with his plans to woo her back into his life permanently.

'You've already been thinking about this?' she asked suspiciously.

'I've done more than think about it. I spoke to your consultant yesterday, and he's comfortable with you flying out there now that your symptoms have eased. He's spoken to an Italian colleague who is willing to have you under his team's care while we're there. We will take every precaution—I've spoken to Lucy and she is happy to travel with us.' Lucy was Marnie's favourite member of the nursing team.

'It seems you've spoken to everyone about it except me,' she commented, her tone dry.

'I didn't want to build your hopes up in case the consultant said it was too great a risk, but we are talking about it now. Just think how much better you'll feel when you're able to breathe some fresh air and take a refreshing swim in the pool,' he coaxed.

Marnie turned her stare away from Domenico's expectant gaze and looked out over the pouring rain. Her heart was racing as quickly as her mind, her hold on her book tight as she found herself filled with a longing to lose herself in the lush grounds of his Italian villa and feel the sun on her face. It hadn't stopped raining since she'd felt well enough to venture outside. She was sick of being confined indoors.

What difference did it make if she continued her recovery here or there? It wasn't like she would be taking a holiday with him. Domenico would spend his days working in his Rome office, so in that regard, there wouldn't be any change to being here at all, and it might just be what she needed to rejuvenate her body and spirits and make her well enough to finally return to her own home.

So what was making her hesitate?

Domenico.

She didn't trust him an inch. He didn't do anything that wasn't for his benefit. She didn't deny that he'd been great these past eight weeks and had kept his word about not discussing their future, but he hadn't needed to. She'd been under his roof, exactly where he wanted her. That she was now on the road to recovery meant he would be looking to restart the game to make her temporary stay a permanent one, and with the stakes being so high…

When he judged the time was right, he would pounce, and she would find herself under a full-throttled offence aimed solely at making her capitulate and tie her life back to his. That time was ticking closer. He would use their child as a weapon. Nothing would be off the table.

But she was stronger than she'd ever given herself credit for. She'd found the courage to break her own heart and leave him, and had fortified her spine with steel to get through the awful months of their divorce. She'd found the strength to tell him to leave after that one heavenly night of weakness…

She cut the memory away.

The only time her strength faltered was when she replayed that night, and she couldn't afford to falter. Not with Domenico. Any weakness would be pounced on.

He didn't want her. That's what she needed to keep fresh in her mind. His antics during their divorce had never been about her; that had been his pride lashing out, and now she was just the incubator who carried his longed-for child.

She'd stopped being the Marnie he respected and valued the day he married her.

Turning her stare back to his, she smiled. 'That's a lovely idea, thank you.'

The flash of triumph in his eyes only confirmed her suspicions about this trip being his first move.

The game had restarted.

She wished her pulse didn't quicken at the thought of where it might lead.

It wouldn't lead anywhere.

It didn't matter what Domenico did or what tricks he thought he had up his sleeves, she would never go back to him.

Marnie had lived alone for six years, but had never felt loneliness like she'd experienced during her short marriage.

CHAPTER FIVE

TWO DAYS LATER, their journey to Rome ran with military precision. Domenico timed everything to perfection. Their 6:00 a.m. start ensured a swift drive to the airport without any delays, and then they were straight on his jet, their flight landing to coincide with the end of Rome's morning rush hour. They were door-to-door within four hours, and Marnie was grateful for it. The travelling had been the only aspect of their trip to concern her, but her first anti-sickness jab in ten days, plentiful sips of water and trusted bland snacks throughout the journey had kept the nausea at bay.

She was lucky. Having done her own research on her condition, Marnie knew many pregnant women with it suffered the whole of the pregnancy. A month into her second trimester and hers was easing by the day. By the time they returned to London, she would be strong enough to go home, she was certain of it, and there was nothing that Domenico could do or say to stop her.

For now, though, she was determined to enjoy her time in his seventeenth-century villa. She loved everything about it.

Nestled in magnificent sprawling grounds in the

foothills of *monteverde*, the green mountain, away from the bustle of Rome proper, it was reputed to have been designed with assistance from Giovanni Grimaldi. A light sand colour, it had a five-storey central block from which three-storey wings spread out, its façade adorned with grand sculptures, the windows all topped with busts in hollowed roundels. When you approached it, you could practically see Roman history coming to life before you.

When Marnie had worked for Domenico, their time had been spent pretty equally between London, Frankfurt, Rome, Washington and New York. Domenico had homes in all those cities. Marnie and his other personal staff stayed in staff apartments, but when he did in-home entertaining, she was always expected to attend in her faithful supervisory capacity (although she'd never been quite certain *what* she was supposed to be supervising, considering all his homes had a full complement of live-in staff). That had all stopped when they'd married. The only travelling she'd done with him had been an extended two-month break in his home city of Rome.

Marnie had learned a great deal about the villa's history and architecture during that two-month stay, mainly because after a month of dedicated sightseeing, there had been little else left for her to do. She'd seen little of her husband but had fallen madly in love with his city and villa.

The household staff who greeted them were the same faces she'd known for years. Making the transition from personal assistant to wife had never felt more awkward than when dealing with people who'd once considered her a colleague. Now that she'd transitioned to ex-wife, she felt the awkwardness even more keenly. Here, in Rome, that awkwardness was compounded by the household staff being so very Italian.

The English staff had adopted a 'nothing to see here' approach to her temporary return. It was as if the six months she'd been gone had never happened. The Italian staff, on the other hand, were avid with curiosity, their stares continuously dipping to her stomach. There was warmth in their curious stares, though, especially when Domenico disappeared to make a phone call, the sense they were welcoming home an old friend, which in turn put Marnie at ease and put the few doubts she'd had about whether coming to Rome was the right thing to bed.

It was a feeling that followed her a short while later when she stepped into her bedroom, a gorgeous space with a four-poster bed and frescoed ceiling…and then fell away when she saw the adjoining door.

She stared at it with mounting horror. How on earth had she forgotten about *that*?

It was around their time in Rome that the frequency of Domenico's visits to her bed had started to increase from a couple of times a week to most nights, and suddenly she was hit with the memory of falling asleep after he'd had sex with her and then being woken around the time the sun had started rising by the adjoining door opening. The mattress had dipped, the sheets rippled, and she'd been gently taken into his strong arms. His mouth had found hers, and with the sensation that they were both in a waking dream, she'd dove her fingers into his soft hair, wrapped her legs around him and welcomed his possession. It had been slow and tender and exquisitely beautiful, and when he left her bed afterwards, it had been with a lingering kiss goodbye.

It was a coupling that had never been spoken of or repeated. Not repeated like that. Sex between them had returned to its usual detached but pleasurable exchange of orgasms. Their marriage had continued in its usual non-affectionate, non-emotional way.

For a long time, Marnie had wondered if she'd dreamed it.

A dream or not, it had been the beginning of the end for her. She'd had the tiniest glimpse of heaven, a taste of what their marriage could be like. Every coupling that came after it sliced a fresh wound into her heart.

No point in letting the memories slice her now, she reasoned, wiping away tears that had sprung from nowhere and inhaling deeply. This was Domenico's territory far more than London was. This was the place he called home, and she needed to be on her guard, not slip into melancholy.

The view from her room was every bit as beautiful as the interior, and she climbed onto a windowsill to look out and centre herself into the here and now.

Domenico's lands seemed to stretch forever. Craning her head to the right, she glimpsed the gorgeous hedged maze. Behind it, out of view, was the villa's private chapel, behind which ran the wall with the secret door into the secret garden. So secret was the garden that she'd only discovered its existence the day before they'd returned to London, and she vowed to explore it this time, while she had the chance.

The tap on her main door pulled her away from her secret garden thoughts. Assuming it was one of the staff with the cup of decaffeinated tea she'd asked for, she pulled a smile to her face and called, 'Come in.'

The smile fell when Domenico strode in.

Unprepared for his appearance in her bedroom and with the memories of that dreamlike early morning still fresh, Marnie's heart slammed. In an instant, the pounding ripples spread through her veins, and her world teetered.

Helpless to stop her gaze locking onto his, her eyes travelled the heartbreakingly gorgeous face she'd once loved with the whole fibre of her being, dipping to the sensuous lips that only once in the whole of their marriage had kissed her with emotion, and suddenly she could *feel* the memory of that lingering caress from that dreamlike early morning. Feel his mouth on hers. Smell the musk of his skin. Feel the texture of his soft hair on her fingers…

Her world hadn't just teetered, it had stopped; a stretched beat of time where all that existed was Domenico.

The stretched beat broke with a snap when he moved from the doorway towards her.

It shouldn't be possible for her heart to race any faster, but the closer each step took him to her, the quicker it cantered until he reached her, and it was nothing but a burr.

'How are you feeling after all that travelling?' he asked, holding her cup out to her.

Painfully aware of the burn of colour staining her cheeks, it took everything she had to keep her hands steady as she took the cup from him, careful not to allow the slightest brush of their fingers.

She had to swallow to say, 'A little tired but okay.' One thing she never did was lie to him about her physical health. The baby in her belly was Domenico's every bit as much as it was hers. He needed the reassurance that everything was okay as much as she did.

He leaned into the wall by the window. 'That's good.' His light brown eyes were watchful. 'You'll rest today?'

She nodded and wished he hadn't chosen to stand so close to her. Domenico hadn't worn cologne since he'd realised literally every scent made her nauseous, but this close, she could smell the fresh cleanliness of his warm skin, and instead of turning her stomach, it turned her heart inside out with longing.

'I'll take it easy, don't worry. You're going to work?' That he'd changed into a tailored navy suit since their arrival pointed to that being the case, and she wished disappointment didn't pang so sharply at the thought of him leaving the villa. She *wanted* him to go. She'd only agreed to come to Rome on the unspoken assumption he'd spend his waking hours setting the world of corporate law alight.

He pulled a face, then grinned before casually saying, 'I'll be back early evening. Dine with me tonight?'

She experienced another sensation of her heart turning inside out before memories of the hundred-odd meals they'd shared crowded into her head.

When they'd first married, Marnie had dressed up for dinner, even applied a little makeup, but if he'd noticed the effort she made, he gave no sign of it, certainly never mentioned it. After months of effort, she'd stopped bothering and had been utterly unsurprised when he'd failed to notice that too.

He'd been great company throughout all those meals, though, but in exactly the way he'd been great company when he'd been her boss. And, just as when he'd been her boss, there hadn't been an ounce of intimacy. Her years-old fantasy of Domenico gazing at her lovingly and occasionally spooning food into her mouth had, like the rest of her fantasies about him, trampled into the dust.

Hating how those memories still had the power to hurt her, she looked back out of the window and with only a hint of snide in her politeness, said, 'I don't want to lose what little appetite I've found, so I'll eat in here, thanks.'

Amusement laced his voice. 'That is, of course, your prerogative. If you decide you've had enough of eating alone, you know where I'll be.'

'I'm perfectly happy in my own company, but thanks.'

His low rumble of laughter soaked through her skin, lancing her as deeply as the memories.

Marnie had always adored Domenico's laugh. If she turned her head, she knew she'd find his brown eyes crinkled with the lines that always appeared around them when he laughed or smiled.

Of everything she'd missed about him, his smile had come top. Being on the receiving end of it was like being hit by a burst of the sun's rays, and suddenly she was hit with another memory, of waking in his arms that particular morning and finding his eyes crinkled in a way she'd never seen before. She'd been hit with such a huge dose of his sunlight that she'd had to scramble away from it and turn her back on him before he blinded her again. Emotions she could barely contain had swirled and bubbled with force enough to choke her, amongst them a deep horror and shame of how she'd behaved before they'd thrown themselves into each other's arms.

Remembering that loss of control over her emotions had been terrifying.

She'd needed him gone then, and she needed him gone now because she could feel those emotions afresh, not the anger but the bubbling and swirling contained in them; the last remnants of the love she'd held for him for so long refusing to die.

'I'm sure if you tell yourself that enough times, you'll come to believe it,' he said knowingly before she heard his footsteps cross the stone floor away from her.

The door opened and closed, and the footsteps vanished.

When Marnie heard the knock on her door three mornings later, she pretended to be asleep.

Even though it was the main door and not the adjoining door being knocked on, her instinct that it was Domenico was proved right when she heard the tread of his steps and breathed in the fresh scent of his shower gel. She kept herself perfectly still, just as she'd done the last two mornings, even when she heard him place her breakfast tray on her table. She could only be grateful he couldn't hear her heart. The roar it was making would prove in an instant that she was faking.

As she'd done yesterday and the day before, she counted to one hundred after he closed the door before getting out of bed.

Her breakfast was the usual two slices of toast, an array of condiments to choose from, and a pot of tea.

Sitting on the windowsill, she ate slowly and methodically, knowing not to rush it. She felt more like her old self than she'd done in months and would not do anything that might encourage the nausea to return. It was a picture-perfect day out there, and now that Domenico had left for work, she was ready to get out there and breathe the fresh air into her lungs.

After a quick shower, she donned a pair of jeans and a pretty white button-down top. It was the first time in months that she'd dared wear jeans, the material too constricting against her belly to risk it aggravating the nausea, and now she was awed to find they were too tight to do up.

A look profile-on in the mirror proved what her jeans were telling her. She'd developed a little bump, and for the first time in so, so long, she smiled. Properly smiled.

Pressing her hand to it, she was awed all over again

to find her skin had tightened, almost like it had shrink-wrapped itself over the baby to protect it, and it hit home to her, truly hit home, that this little bump contained her baby. That was her baby in there, nestled in the safety of her belly. Somehow, they'd both got through the worst of her illness. They were both still there, and she felt an almost overwhelming urge to call Domenico and tell him to come back so he could see it for himself. He would be as thrilled to see the bump as she was, and before she could stop it, a wave of misery sluiced through the joy to know they would never share the joy of their child together the way their child deserved.

But their child deserved every chance at safety and happiness. Marnie had lived through the hell of parents who hated each other, and she would never put her child through it. It had been terrifying when her father walked out and she'd been left alone with her drunken mother, but at least she'd been able to sleep at night without being woken by their screaming rows. At least she hadn't needed to hide in her wardrobe anymore.

She might not be able to give her child a two-parent family, but she would love and protect it to her dying breath. Domenico would too. They just couldn't do it together, and she had to pray that one day he would accept it and stop fighting.

Deciding to keep the jeans on, she left the buttons undone—the way they fit at her hips meant there was no danger of them falling down—and headed down the stone stairs. After grabbing a bottle of water from the kitchen, she slipped out of the villa's rear.

The villa's grounds were split into clearly defined areas, and it was to the intricate rose garden that Marnie headed. Created hundreds of years ago in imitation of the rose gardens beloved of the English royalty, in its centre was a beautiful marble fountain of the goddess Venus rising out of a pearlescent scallop shell.

The wall of the fountain's basin was a couple of feet high. After removing her sandals, Marnie sat astride it before twisting round to dip her feet in the refreshing water, and tilted her face to the sun.

Eyes closed, she breathed the clean, fragrant air deep into her lungs and imagined the sun's rays penetrating her flesh, injecting her with its energy, and as she imagined it, she felt it, tiny electric tingles dancing on her skin.

'I thought I'd find you here.'

So startled was she at the unexpected sound of Domenico's voice that she lost her balance, would have tipped backwards and crashed onto the gravelled ground if his super-quick reflexes hadn't seen him whip an arm out to catch her.

'Steady,' he murmured, gently righting her. 'My apologies. I didn't mean to scare you.'

Her heart pounding at both the shock of his appearance and the shock of his touch, she splayed her hands on the wall either side of her thighs and tried her hardest to catch her breath. 'I didn't hear you coming.'

'That was obvious.' He sat beside her, but facing the other way. 'You were lost in your own little world.' She heard the smile in his voice. 'It looked a very peaceful world.'

'It was.' She swallowed more air into her lungs. 'Why aren't you at work?'

'I'm taking the day off.'

She closed her eyes. 'Why?'

'Because I'm not going to get very far in convincing you to come back to me if we don't spend any time together. This is our fourth day here, and I've seen nothing of you, not with me working all day and you refusing to spend time with me in the evenings. We need to talk, Marnie.'

'I *knew* it.' Shaking her head, she gave a bitter laugh. 'I knew that coming here was you making your first move.'

'And yet still you came.'

Unable to deny it, she sighed. Marnie had known from the off that Domenico was going to use their time in Rome to start the game again. 'Is this where you tell me you've stolen my passport and plan to keep me locked up until I agree to remarry you?'

He chuckled lightly. 'It is a tempting thought, *fiore mio*, but no.'

She squeezed her eyes. 'It's way too late to start with endearments, and what does that even mean?'

'*Fiore mio*? It translates as my flower. It felt an appropriate endearment, seeing as we're sitting in a rose garden.'

'There are no appropriate endearments between us, Dom. That ship has sailed.'

'I don't believe that.'

'You need to start believing it. I will never come back to you.'

'You would deprive our child of being raised by two parents in a committed marriage?'

Anger unfurling, she whipped her stare to him. 'I knew you'd do that too, try to weaponise our child against me, so don't. We both want what's best for it, and I know this much—what we had was no marriage.'

She waited for his usual denials and arguments. Waited for him to tell her what an excellent husband he'd been and how she'd had everything money could buy lavished on her. Waited for him to make the usual implications that she was a selfish, unreasonable, ungrateful witch.

After a long moment passed, he expelled a long breath. 'What if I told you I have given much thought to what you said about my failings as a husband, and that I am prepared to make the changes you want?'

So stunned was Marnie at his words that she wasn't sure she hadn't misheard him.

'Since you told me about the baby, my perspective has changed.' He shifted slightly, his arm brushing against hers with the movement, but he kept his stare fixed forward. 'I am still angry at how you left me and angry that you waited for the divorce to be finalised before taking the pregnancy test, but the baby is more important than my anger. I will never accept being a part-time father, and I am prepared to make all the changes you require to bring you back to me and make our marriage work. But it has to come from you, too—in the year we lived together, you never told me you were unhappy. I knew nothing about how you were feeling until the night you left me.'

Taken aback at how he'd so quickly and neatly turned it onto her, Marnie's mouth dropped open in disbelief.

'Why didn't you talk to me?' he asked into the stunned silence. 'Why didn't you tell me how you felt? You walked away without giving me the opportunity to make things better for you.'

Bitterness rose so sharply she could taste it on her tongue. 'This is so you, Dom,' she said shakily, turning her stare back to the marble Venus. 'After all this time, you finally hold your hands up and admit to being a lousy husband and then in the next breath put the blame back on me.'

'That is not what I'm doing.' A hint of anger now laced his oh-so-reasonable voice. 'I'm saying that we have spent all this time blaming each other for the destruction of our marriage when we both need to accept that we each played our part in it.' He paused, shifting his weight again, and she imagined him stretching his long legs out in the way she'd seen him do a thousand times.

'You know,' he continued, 'I have spent much of the last eight weeks scheming ways to force you back to me, but I have also thought a lot about a photo I found in your flat when I was collecting your clothes. It's the photo in your bedroom of you as a little girl. Do you know, I know nothing of your childhood? I don't even know who the woman in the photo with you is.

'You have been one of the most important people in my life for over seven years, and I don't know you. We've never talked, Marnie, not about anything that mattered, and I accept responsibility for much of that. You know I like to keep the personal separate from the professional in the workplace, and then when we married, I had the perfect marriage set out in my mind. I set the tone to make it what I needed it to be, but I accept now that it is not the marriage you need it to be, and I am willing to make the changes so it's a marriage you can be happy in, but it can't just come from me. We need to know each other better so we can better understand each other, and if you're unhappy about something, you need to tell me, not hide it.'

Marnie unscrewed her bottle of water, needing to quench her suddenly bone-dry throat. Her hand was trembling so hard that she missed her mouth and sloshed water down her chin. Rubbing the water away, she forced herself to calm down. Her head was reeling, a hope she tried desperately to contain smashing in her chest.

After a more successful attempt at quenching her thirst, she quietly said, 'When you say you're prepared to make the changes I need to be happy…what changes are you thinking of?'

Domenico might have chosen not to bother getting to know her, but she knew him, and she knew how his mind worked. He would have written a mental checklist of the things she was unhappy about and then written the perfect solution beside each one.

'I'm talking specifically about your unhappiness at feeling like you were only wanted as a baby-making machine and not as a person in your own right—I think I am right in saying everything stems from that. To mitigate this, I am willing for us to share a bedroom. When I travel on business, I am willing for you to accompany me whenever you wish. I have never cheated on you and am willing to promise to continue being faithful. I will also carve more time in my schedule for you and delegate more at work so we can take proper breaks together, and when we do take those breaks, I will consult with you about where we go.'

A burst of despairing laughter rose up her throat as the bloom of hope faded. He could have had a clipboard to tick off the solutions.

Marnie gazed into Venus's marble eyes and, as foolish as she knew it to be, wished she were real. Wished what she represented was real.

'You make it sound like a business negotiation,' she said when she could speak without her voice breaking. 'But what about love, Dom? Where does that fit with your plan to bring me back into your life for good?'

CHAPTER SIX

DOMENICO DREW IN a deep breath and closed his eyes, remembering the night Marnie left him and the sadness in her eyes when she'd said, 'I want a marriage built on love, Dom. We haven't even got a marriage built on friendship…'

His mind skipped forward six months, to the night he turned up at her flat and his last-ditch attempt to talk sense into her that had ended in a screaming match. He'd never heard her raise her voice before, not even mildly, but she'd been right in his face, shouting at him. 'If you think I'm going back to that loveless joke of a marriage, then it's you who's lost your mind, not me! I would have given you everything, but you didn't want it—you never wanted it because you never wanted *me*!'

'Of course I wanted you!' he'd roared. 'I wouldn't have married you if I didn't want you!'

'You wanted what my body could give you, not what *I* could give you!' she'd screamed. 'I was just a walking, talking baby-making machine to you.'

'A baby-making machine would have had more life to it than you ever did!'

'Only because you sucked all the life out of me!'

'*I* sucked the life out of you? Screwing you was like screwing a wind-up doll!'

'Well, being screwed by you was like being fucked by an android with only one setting, and it wasn't a wife-pleasuring one!'

In all the years he'd known Marnie, he'd never heard her swear, not even mildly, and he had no idea if it was hearing such an oath so viciously delivered from a mouth usually so calm that tipped him over the edge or if it was that by that point, their faces were so close they were breathing in each other's fury, but it was the last insult either gave that night as a breath later their mouths had fused. In an instant, they'd been kissing with the same fury they'd been feeding to each other through their hate and clawing at each other's clothes.

He'd pushed her against the only available wall space. Her hands had gone straight to his trousers to free him, his hand groping the knickers beneath her dress and ripping them off her. Barely a minute could have passed since she'd called him an android before he'd lifted her up the wall and thrust himself inside her.

He'd been possessed. They had both been.

It had been the most incredible night of his life. Only one night…morning…had come close. A different kind of possession. Here in Rome. He'd dreamed of her, a vivid dream that had propelled him out of his bed before he was fully awake, a dreamlike state enveloping him as he'd slipped into her room and slipped beneath her sheets. He hadn't been capable of detaching his mind. Hadn't even tried.

That first possession had been easy to dismiss from

his mind. The second possession had been impossible. That he'd woken the next morning with all those damned emotions in him was too disturbing to think of in any depth, and once he'd got over the gut punch of Marnie's rejection, he'd been glad to walk away from her, glad to know they were over. Their marriage was never supposed to be about feelings. He didn't want them.

Emotions were destructive, and what he'd felt for Marnie that night; the passion that had driven him… driven them both…was deeper than anything he'd ever felt for Carmela.

But through the second possession that had come within a breath of shattering his world, their baby had been created, and if he wanted to be the full-time father he'd always envisaged himself being and for his child to have the life it deserved, then he needed to make Marnie see reason and come back to him.

'I know what you want to hear, but I've never lied to you and I'm not going to start now,' he said slowly, focusing his stare on the three bees buzzing happily over the rambling rosebush in front of him, gorging on the last of the year's pollen. 'I married Carmela for what I believed was love, and she left me for my oldest friend. She left me two weeks after my father died. That's what romantic love gave me. Now I feel nothing for her. The love, if that's what it was, died.

'The only love in a marriage that's indestructible is the love of the parents for their children, and we already love our child, and it's for that love that I will be the husband you need me to be. Our marriage *will* be based on love, Marnie: our love for our child, and to give our child the stability that is every child's right. I will do my best to be the husband you want me to be. My parents had a marriage built on mutual respect and the deepest of affection, and that's what we can build too, but to build it, we both need to commit to putting our child's needs first.'

He sounded so *reasonable*, Marnie thought despairingly. Everything Domenico touched turned to gold, and now he'd convinced himself he could apply the same mindset and make their marriage a golden one.

'But I *am* putting our child's needs first,' she said. 'If I thought I could spend the next twenty years in a loveless marriage, then I would do it and then try and find love when our baby's all grown up, but I *can't*.'

An edge came into his voice. 'I've just explained why it won't be loveless, but ultimately it comes down to mindset. If we both make a concerted effort to provide stability and unity, then we can raise a happy child within the confines of a stable and committed marriage.'

Another bubble of despairing laughter tickled her throat. If only she didn't know him so well she could probably talk herself into falling in line with his plans and going back to him.

'Our baby is going to be spoiled for love from both of us whether we're together or not, but if I come back to you…'

It came to Marnie that the way they were sitting, shoulder to shoulder but facing opposite directions, was like a human version of Janus, and just as one of the faces of the Roman god was turned to the past and the other to the future, it seemed to her that that's how they were faced, too. Domenico had their future all mapped out, while all she could see was the past.

'Do you have any idea how damaging it is to a child to be raised in a home filled with hate and resentment?' she asked tremulously. 'Because I do. My parents barely knew each other when I was conceived, and all I remember of my early years before my father left is the fights and abuse. They stayed together for my sake and ended up destroying each other. I watched them break each other, and I will not put our child through that.'

'I'm sorry you lived through that, but answer me this—when, in all the years we worked together and the year we lived together, did we ever fight or abuse each other?'

Now she did laugh. 'We didn't work together, Dom. You were my boss. My job was to make sure your working life ran as smoothly as it could, and when we lived together, it was in your home and under your rules. I bent my life to your will, but the minute I left, you turned me into your enemy and treated me like some corporate opponent who had to be defeated.'

The edge in his voice sharpened. 'I was fighting to make you see sense and come back to me.'

'Again, you're making it all about *you*, and you didn't want *me* back; you wanted the pliable Marnie who bent herself to your will to come back because you hated that she'd slipped out from under your thumb. You say you want to get to know me, yet I just shared something about my past, and you showed no curiosity about it other than in how it affects you.'

There was a sharp inhalation of breath, but before he could defend himself, she continued, speaking quicker than she usually did in her need to get the words out. 'My guess is Carmela did way more damage than you want to admit because you don't do feelings at all, not yours or other people's. You hide from them. Do you think it escaped my attention that all your efforts to win me back were dropped straight after that night in my flat? You walked out, and I never heard from you or saw you again.'

'You told me to leave,' he bit out.

'And didn't you prove me right to do that. How we both behaved that night…' She swallowed. 'I've never lost control like that before, and it frightens me that I was capable of behaving like that and saying such cruel things, and then what came off the back of it…' She had to swallow again, trying desperately to drive away the images of their wild lovemaking, and fighting with everything she had to keep her voice even when her heart was such a thrashing mess.

All those years she'd spent dreaming of Domenico making passionate love to her, and then when the passion of her dreams had finally sprung to life, it had been driven by hate and fury.

'I think that in the cold light of day, it was the same for you, too,' she continued shakily. 'We set something off in each other that night, and I am as sure as I've ever been sure about anything that if either of us had known something like that could explode between us, you would never have asked me to marry you, and I would never have said yes.' For him, it was the loss of control when their passion had exploded, because he *had* lost control in a way he'd never come close to in the whole of their marriage. For Marnie, it was what had come before it. The fury. The viciousness. Like the ghost of her mother had taken control of her mouth. 'If not for the baby, you would have been happy to never see me again.'

Only the tinkling of water from the Venus fountain cut through the silence that followed.

Slowly, Marnie twisted back around so she was facing the same direction as Domenico. He'd become as still as the marble Venus.

Hands shaking, she picked up her sandals and got unsteadily to her feet. The whole of her body was shaking.

'It's getting too hot out here, so I'm going back in,' she said without looking at him. 'I don't want to fight you, Dom. I never did. I just want to live my life peacefully and for our child to have that same peace too.'

Back in the villa, Marnie went straight to her room. The peace she craved seemed a long way away. The adrenaline that had carried her through that awful but necessary talk with Domenico had barely lessened in the walk back, and she paced the room, unable to settle in body or mind.

She would have happily lived the rest of her life never thinking of that night again, never mind talk about it, but now that it had been brought up between them, it played as vividly in her head as if she were living it all again.

The intensity of the emotions and feelings she'd experienced that night was terrifying to remember. The violence of her emotions. The way she'd screamed at him.

It was like the coil of her misery that had wound tighter and tighter during her marriage and the awful months that followed, months where her hate for him had grown in direct proportion to the depth of how badly she missed him, had snapped, and all her suppressed emotions had sprung free.

She'd never wanted to believe herself capable of acting like her mother, and only because she'd spent her life terrified of being anything like her did Marnie refuse to blame her behaviour on the wine she'd been drinking. She knew the alcohol had played its part, wished she'd never given in to the need to numb the pain of the decree nisi, but it had been her mouth that had shouted obscenities at Domenico. Not her mother's. *Her* words. Her actions belonged to her alone.

More shameful was remembering how alive she'd felt in his arms, and as she paced her room, she could feel the embers of the wild hedonism that had possessed her. The passion that had unleashed that night was a passion she'd spent the whole of her marriage aching for, and it hurt unbearably to know that once she'd finally tasted it, it was a passion born of furious hate and not love. His hate and hers.

Her door opened without any warning.

She spun around.

Their eyes caught. Locked.

Her heart swelled into her throat.

His jaw clenched.

His handsome features taut, Domenico reached her in four long strides. There was no time to react before he cupped her cheeks in his giant hands and brought his face down to hers.

'If you think that's the end of the matter, then you don't know me at all,' he ground out harshly. The heat of his breath danced over her skin a beat before his mouth claimed hers, and in the next beat Marnie was lost in a kiss so possessive and demanding that she was helpless to do anything but fall head first into it.

Electricity zinged through her veins, the first sweep of his tongue against hers zinging her senses back to life, and she wrapped her arms tightly around him, devouring his mouth with the same fury he was devouring hers.

The sensation of his fingers diving into her hair to cradle her head as he deepened the kiss was heavenly; every movement of his mouth on hers, every stroke of his tongue, every touch, it all the fed the flame of the ache she'd carried for him for so many years she could barely remember a time when it hadn't lived inside her, and it was only by forcing herself to remember the strength it had taken to walk away and the agony of it all that she was able to wrench her mouth away and push at his chest.

'What are you *doing*?' Her demand came out like a wail.

She'd been scooped into his arms before she even

realised he was swooping to pick her up and carried onto the bed before she could gather the wits to protest. Domenico was a tall and physically intimidating man, but he had the agility of a gymnast, and when he laid her down, his head came down on the pillow beside hers, and she was being spooned into him before she could take a breath.

'Now you listen to me, Marnie Cannavaro,' he said roughly…and yet somehow gently…into the top of her head. 'I don't care what a piece of paper says, you are still my wife. I know I was a terrible husband to you. I am selfish and spoilt, and one of the reasons I chose you as my wife is because I arrogantly assumed you would be happy to continue spoiling me and bending your life to my will—you called that right. I was very much aware that you had a crush on me, and I took advantage of that, but for all my selfishness and arrogance, I chose you because I *like* you. I've always liked you. Mine is a high-pressure life, and your presence brought calm to it. When you took your annual leave, I always felt your absence, and not just because your supersonic brain wasn't on hand when I needed to know something immediately. I missed *you.*

'When I knew it was time for me to remarry, there was no one else, only you, but you're right that if I'd known what exploded between us that night could happen, I would have chosen someone else, and I spent the six weeks after that night determined to forget about you because what happened that night was so far from what I wanted for us you would not believe. But it did happen, Marnie, and we made a baby through it, and

I am prepared to do anything to bring you back to me. I told you the concessions I was prepared to make, but you need to think of them as the opening salvo in a one-sided negotiation that you hold all the cards to.'

There was no loosening of the rigid, too-bony back Domenico's chest was pressed against. And no loosening of the tightness inside his chest or slowing of his thumping heart.

He hadn't meant to kiss her. He hadn't even meant to touch her.

He'd only decided to take the day off work when he'd taken her breakfast into her room and found her pretending to be asleep again. Did she seriously believe he didn't know when she was faking sleep when he'd spent so many hours watching over her these last two months?

Something inside of him had snapped, and he'd decided there and then that he'd had enough. The staff all spoke glowingly about the clear effect the Italian air was having on her and how well she was recovering, but the minute Domenico was home, she hid away in her bedroom and pretended to be asleep. It wasn't like when they'd been in London and he'd been able to use the excuse of watching over the patient to sit in her room every night while she recovered. She was no longer ill. No, Marnie was hiding. From him.

No more hiding, he'd determined. They needed to talk, and that wasn't going to happen unless he forced it.

And so he'd forced it, and then he'd watched her walk back to the villa with so many damned feelings coursing through him. His placid little wife… *Dio*, she saw him more clearly than anyone else ever had, and it was the most unsettling sensation, to be truly seen and to be found wanting. Not even Carmela had made him feel that.

That's when the anger at Marnie's flat refusal to listen and her self-appointed role as his judge, jury and executioner had hit him. She said he only heard what he wanted to hear? Well, what the hell was she doing if not the same thing?

Increasing fury had propelled him to his feet, and he'd followed her into the villa determined to repay her with some home truths of his own because he'd gone out of his way to be gentle in the way he'd pointed out her habit of keeping her unhappiness bottled up. Hell, she kept *everything* bottled up, only letting it out when it was too damned late to do anything about it.

And then he'd barged into her room and she'd spun around to face him and there had been such starkness in her expression that everything he'd angrily psyched himself into letting rip at her had melted away under the weight of emotion that had filled his guts.

Closing his eyes, he inhaled the sweetness of her shampoo and rubbed his nose into the silky tresses. Marnie's scent was as soothing as he used to find her presence, and as he thought of her soothing presence in the past tense, Domenico forced himself to admit that for the two months she'd been back in his life, it had soothed him in a very different way to know she was back under his roof.

Her presence had stopped being soothing the longer

the months of their marriage had passed. It had been such a gradual process he couldn't pinpoint when he'd had to force his good humour in the meals they shared or when going into her bedroom had become an act of torture second only to leaving it.

The torture had come from the unwanted notion that the more he made love to her, the more he wanted to make love to her and the stronger the sense that she was slipping away from him.

He *had* felt her slipping away. It had been there in her responses to his lovemaking, the sensation he was making love only to a body, the mind attached to it closed off and locked away from him. He just hadn't wanted to acknowledge it, had fought against acknowledging that the perfect marriage he'd created as a means of creating a family was cracking.

He'd been cracking too, he acknowledged painfully. His increasing desperation to impregnate her had come because he'd subconsciously known he was losing her. Get her pregnant and then she'd never be able to leave him, that's what his subconscious had demanded, and now she *was* pregnant and still she would rather live in a flat in one of the most dangerous areas of London than come back to him.

But it had been more than desperation to impregnate her that had seen him go to Marnie night after night, and for the first time, he forced himself to consider the possibility that in the long months of their marriage, he'd fallen for his wife.

It was a notion that brought perspiration to his face.

It was just pregnancy hormones, he valiantly assured himself, because there was no way he could have fallen for her, not when he'd spent their whole damned marriage ensuring that didn't happen. Sure, he wasn't the one carrying their child, but he'd spent two months watching Marnie suffer and being unable to do a damned thing to ease it. That had to affect a man. He cared for her and felt protective of her because he wasn't a monster. That didn't mean he needed to look back into the past and start seeing things there that didn't exist.

Closing his eyes even tighter, he filled his lungs again with Marnie's scent and spooned himself even closer so his knees bent into the back of hers. Only the awareness she'd only so recently stopped feeling nauseous at every little thing stopped him tightening his hold around her.

'Give me a week,' he said, breaking the long silence. 'Let me spend this time proving that I can be the husband you want me to be.'

She took so long to respond that he began to think she really had fallen asleep, and when she did speak, her voice was so faint it was barely audible. 'But it won't be real.'

CHAPTER SEVEN

IT HAPPENED SO quickly that Marnie didn't have time to snatch a breath of resistance before she was rolled onto her back with the same swiftness that she'd been scooped into Domenico's arms and laid on the bed.

Propping himself onto his forearm, he glowered down at her. 'I'm doing my best to give you everything you want, and all you have to say is that it isn't real?'

'But it won't be, will it?' As hard as she tried, she couldn't stop the misery reflecting in her voice. Being spooned into him and listening to his rich voice while his breath had danced through her hair and the sensation of their fused mouths still buzzed so deeply on her lips and in her veins…

If he put his hand to her heart, he would know beyond doubt how deeply he affected her, and she wished desperately for a means to numb both her heart and her body to him, wished too, that the longing to slip back into the pretence that had got her through the early months of their marriage wasn't so very strong. 'We'll both know it's fake and that you're just going through the motions and pretending.'

His jaw clenched, nostrils flaring. 'We spend our

lives going through motions, from brushing our teeth to driving a car. Does that make those things any less real?'

She wanted to cry. 'You know what I mean. I can't pretend our marriage is some kind of artificial simulation. Not now.'

'That kiss we just shared felt real. Damned real. That didn't feel artificial or like going through some motion.'

In the beat of a heart, hot colour flooded her face. She wanted to deny that the kiss had been shared, but they would both know her denials were a lie.

She'd never had control of her physical responses to Domenico any more than she had control of her heart.

The intensity of the light brown eyes staring into hers increased, but his jaw loosened, his mouth and voice softening. 'Why did you marry me, Marnie?'

Her heart virtually punched its way through her chest. 'You ask that now, months after we divorced?'

'Do you know why I thought you said yes?'

The colour on her cheeks now at saturation point, she shook her head.

'I knew you had a crush on me, and I thought myself such a great catch that I couldn't see a reason why any woman would say no.'

Taken off guard at such brutal honesty, she gave a small shout of laughter. Oh, that was such a very Domenico thing to say. In all the years she'd known him, he'd never suffered from false modesty. He knew exactly who he was and where he was going, one of the many things that had left her, the girl who'd never dared imagine a future for herself, so awed about him in those early years. She'd never met anyone like him before. Just being in a room with him was intoxicating.

The gorgeously sensual mouth curved into a smile.

Bending his elbow, eyes not breaking the lock between them, he rested his cheek on his palm and gently ran a finger the length of her nose. Quivers of sensation followed his trail.

'The sun's made your freckles come back out,' he murmured. 'I like your freckles. I like that you don't try to hide them.' The smile dimmed. 'I don't like that you try to hide what's on the inside, so tell me, why did you agree to marry me?'

Because I wanted what we are sharing right this very moment, lying on a bed, talking and gazing into each other's eyes, our bodies so close I can feel the heat emanating from you.

Blinking back tears, she whispered, 'You already called it. You were a great catch I already had a crush on.'

He raised a lazy, disbelieving eyebrow. 'We had no pre-nup—you could have screwed me for millions if you'd wanted, but you let me screw you over without fighting back and walked away from our marriage without anything. You're far too intelligent to snare yourself a rich man and walk away with nothing if that was your reason for marrying him, and I know, too, that you wouldn't marry someone because of a crush, so I ask you again, why marry me? What did you want from me that compelled you to say yes?'

'I didn't want anything.'

'If you didn't want anything, then you wouldn't have had any expectations that I failed to reach the mark on.'

Sometimes she really hated how forensically his mind worked. She'd seen it applied so many times over the years in a professional context that the few times he'd tried to apply it to her in the months after she left him, she'd been able to stonewall him. But those other times, they hadn't been lying together on a bed with his face so close to hers that she could see the thick stubble breaking through the skin on his cheeks. Those other times, Domenico's eyes had danced with malicious loathing, not with attentiveness, and whether it was the physical closeness or the intensity, she didn't know, but when she opened her mouth, all that came out was the truth.

'I didn't just have a crush on you, Dom,' she said quietly. 'It was much more than that. When I met you, I'd barely left school. I'd just finished my exams and entered the world of work, and it was terrifying for me. I was surrounded by adults, and frightened of so many things, but the biggest thing was screwing it all up and being fired, and then you swept in when I'd been there only a few days and…' She smiled as the sweet memory filled her head. 'I was the lowest of the low in your workforce—I was literally the most insignificant person there—and you took the time to welcome me, and then you said that I'd impressed you. That made my whole year. It was validation of a kind I'd never known before, and when you chose me, personally, to work on your personal team…that made my *life*. And so I made you my life.'

How could she not have when, after a life spent feeling invisible, this gorgeous, gregarious, wildly successful man hadn't just noticed her but seen something in her that no one had seen before? Something worthwhile. Something worth investing his time and energy into bringing to blossom.

She swallowed, her voice dropping even lower. 'In my eyes, you were akin to a god, and I worshipped you. I would have done anything for you. When you asked me to marry you, it felt like all my dreams had come true, and I was so blinded by my feelings and the pedestal I'd put you on that it took me a long time to realise none of it was real and that my dreams were made of sand and your feet were made of clay.'

The deep crease in his brow made her heart turn over, and without thinking, Marnie rolled onto her side to face him and gently palmed his stubbly cheek. 'You know, saying all that aloud…' A wave of regret and pain caught in her throat. 'It makes me see that none of this was your fault. It was mine. You never lied to me. My expectations and hopes were all mine, and I married you with dreams no human could live up to, because all I ever wanted from our marriage was for you to be my Prince Charming.'

Tears filled her eyes as the depth of her naivety rang clear for the first time. 'I wanted the fairy tale,' she whispered. 'I wanted to be rescued like the princess from a fairy tale and smothered with love and for you to put me on the same pedestal I'd had you on for all those years. I knew you didn't do love and romance, and yet still I let those dreams live and breathe. You made it very plain that you were marrying me only because you wanted children, but I closed my ears. I let myself believe what I wanted to believe.' What she'd needed to believe.

He cleared his throat before hoarsely asking, 'What did you want rescuing from?'

She gave a tiny, helpless shrug. 'My life.' And as she made the confession she barely comprehended herself, she felt a movement in her belly that made her snatch her hand from his cheek and roll onto her back to lift her top and touch her little bump.

Alarm flashed in the light brown eyes. 'Are you okay?'

She nodded, a dazed smile breaking out. How lucky that she'd kept her jeans on and left them unbuttoned! 'I can feel…' She groped for his hand and guided it to the spot on the lower part of her abdomen where she could feel the fluttering and pressed down.

'Can you feel it?' She rested her hand on his searching fingers as excitement of such purity she felt like she could float to the ceiling skipped through her.

His face a mask of concentration, he shook his head. 'It's our baby?'

'Yes.' Her smile widened. 'It feels like tiny ripples beneath my skin.' She sighed as the flutters faded away and nuzzled her head closer to his. 'It's stopped. I'm sorry you didn't feel it.'

His face broke into a smile. 'Seeing your reaction was en…' He cut himself off, his eyes suddenly widening. Spreading his fingers out over her belly, he gently smoothed them over the skin. 'You have a bump.'

Euphoric at feeling her baby's movements for the first time, she laughed. 'Yes.'

She could feel as well as see his awe as he continued to run his hand over the bump cocooning their baby, and when he lifted himself to place a tender kiss on her swelling stomach, it felt like the most natural thing in the world, so natural that the tears that had been threatening to fall since he'd joined her in the rose garden finally spilled over.

When he looked back at her, his brow creased again, the lines even deeper than before. 'What's wrong?'

Too choked to speak, she shook her head and lifted her arms to him.

He didn't hesitate, lying back beside her and gathering her to him.

She twisted into him, holding him tightly as she rested her cheek on the warm solidity of his chest and let the silent tears flow. She didn't even know what she was crying for but the way Domenico was holding her and stroking her hair gave more comfort than she would have believed.

How many times during their marriage had she longed to be just *held* like this?

'I'm sorry,' she whispered when the tears had finally dried up. 'I got a little overwhelmed there.'

The arms holding her tightened.

Frightened at how good and right this felt, she disentangled her arms and lifted her upper body.

The moment their eyes locked back together, her heart shuddered.

Slowly, Domenico lifted himself upright too, until his face was only inches from hers.

They stayed like that for the longest time, neither of them speaking or moving, just staring at each other in an unspoken language that made her want to cry again. But there were no more tears. Domenico captured a lock of fallen hair and tucked it behind her ear before his mouth closed in on hers and captured it.

If his kiss had been as furiously demanding as the one they'd shared when he'd stormed into her room, she would have pushed him away. But it wasn't. It was achingly, *achingly* tender.

The tips of his fingers pressed into her cheek, and then he moved his mouth slowly, so slowly, over hers, and gently drew her lips apart.

Closing her eyes, Marnie sank into it. Her senses infusing with the musky scent of his skin, she met the unhurried stroke of his silken tongue and dreamily drank in the exotic darkness of his taste.

Mouths and tongues entwined, the flame of desire that had never died for him flickered as his fingers slid from her cheek and threaded through her hair. His other hand slipped behind her back and dipped beneath her top to rest on her naked flesh, igniting a thrill of sensation, gently pulling her closer to him.

At the first touch of her tender breasts against his muscular chest, another, deeper, thrill of sensation lazily uncoiled, and she sank even deeper into the kiss, so deep that their faces became meshed together and all conscious thought was lost because *she* was lost.

She had no idea which of them broke it. One moment she was lost in the most beautiful kiss of her life, the next she was dazedly gazing again into Domenico's eyes with no recollection of winding an arm around his neck or of how her legs came to be over his lap. Her heart…she could feel the pounding of its beat *everywhere.*

His jaw clenched, and his shoulders rose as he took a deep inhalation. But his eyes stayed on hers, and when he opened his mouth, she had a flash of intuition of what he was going to say and pressed a finger to his lips with a shake of her head. 'Don't,' she whispered. 'Please, don't say anything.'

Marnie couldn't bear for the kiss she'd spent the whole of her life waiting for or that joyous moment when their baby had come fully alive for them to be used as a weapon. Couldn't bear to hear confirmation that their kiss had come with an ulterior purpose rather than from the pure emotion that had driven her part in it.

She swallowed. 'I'm willing to try.'

His eyes narrowed, the groove in his forehead making another appearance. But he didn't speak. Not with his mouth.

'You're right,' she said, even as a part of her shrivelled in fear of the future pain she was going to unleash on herself. 'Our baby does deserve to be raised with two committed parents, and if you're willing to try, then so am I.' She attempted a smile. 'You've shared the bad side of the pregnancy with me, and it's only fair you share the good side too. If that flutter I felt is any indication, then there's going to be lots of the good side to share.' And now that she'd experienced the joy of that flutter and felt the life behind, how could she deny Domenico the chance to share the rest of it?

The baby in her belly didn't belong to her alone; it belonged to them both. It needed them both. As much as Marnie had hated the hell of living with parents who despised the air the other breathed, at least they'd tried. Who was to say her life wouldn't have been worse if they hadn't? What would have become of her if her father hadn't made that initial effort before abandoning them?

Domenico would never love her, but if she tried hard enough, maybe she could learn to live with it rather than hate him for it. Maybe he was right, and all that was needed was a change of mindset to make it work, because he was right that their child deserved it, and unlike Marnie's father, Domenico would never leave it. He would be there for it, loving it, every day of its life.

Their child deserved for them to at least try. That it had fully introduced itself when they were together made her think their baby wanted that too.

She put her finger back to his lips before he could speak. 'But, Dom, I'm sorry, I won't marry you again. I need to know that if…' When… 'it doesn't work out, I can walk away, and I need you to promise that if that happens, you won't fight it.'

The light brown eyes that hadn't broken from hers glittered, the sensuous lips pulling in as his features tightened. 'Our child deserves the security of marriage.'

'And I deserve the security of knowing I can walk

away and that you'll let me go. You said that I held all the negotiating cards; well, this is me playing them, and I'm doing my best to play them in a way that's fair to all of us, our baby included.'

The longest time passed before he closed his eyes and expelled a long breath. When he next met her stare, a wry smile played on his lips. 'You know, you would make one hell of a litigator.'

She tried not to let her chest inflate too hard at his compliment, but she'd always been a sucker for any hint of praise from him, had loved nothing more than having her hard work recognised, which he'd done frequently. She would not let it turn her head now. 'Does that mean you accept my terms?'

The wry smile remained. 'I don't see that I have any choice.'

'And you promise that you won't fight me if I choose to walk away?'

His eyes narrowed with thought. Slowly, he said, 'I will make that promise if you make a promise in return—that if ever you feel you want to walk away, you talk to me first and let me try to fix whatever it is that's making you feel the need to leave.'

A stab of guilt pierced her chest.

Would things have been different if she'd told him how she felt before she'd left him? She didn't know because she'd never given him the chance, something that made the guilt morph into shame.

All those long, lonely months maintaining the fiction of being the perfect wife for him while living with increasing misery, resentment and loathing, and not once giving voice to it…

Why was that? Why had she only found her voice once she'd made up her mind to leave?

'I can agree to that,' she whispered.

A pulse on his jaw throbbed, and he slowly inclined his head. 'Then I accept your terms.'

A sensation that was a cross between sickness and excitement exploded inside her, a sensation so familiar to how she'd reacted when Domenico had proposed that she came within a whisker of saying she'd changed her mind and demanding to return to England. Those old feelings had been on a hiding to nothing from the start.

But there would be no changing of her mind. She might have no faith that they could make it work, but they owed it to their child to try, she saw that now. It was all about mindset, just as Domenico had said, and this time her mindset would be that she was entering their arrangement with her love blinkers off and her eyes wide open.

Except it was a hard mindset to maintain when her legs were still draped over his lap and her hand was still cupping his neck and his hand was still touching the naked flesh of her back and he was staring at her with such an intense but unreadable expression.

A new form of sickness rose inside her, another that was painfully familiar, this one anticipation as she held her breath and waited for what came next.

Would he seal their agreement with another kiss? Seal it with something more…?

The anticipation accelerated. Her pulse cantering, Marnie found herself suddenly struggling to breathe.

Eyes still boring into hers, he traced the contour of her ear with a finger. 'Are you hungry?'

Another emotion lanced her, one as familiar and powerful as all the others that had caught her in their grip since he'd joined her in the rose garden. Disappointment.

He was talking about food.

Mindset, Marnie, she valiantly reminded herself, as what she'd just agreed to flashed before her.

Sex in their marriage had only ever been about making a baby. Their baby's actual conception had been an aberration fuelled by bitter anger and rage-unleashed alcohol, one she knew he would never allow to be repeated. The kiss when he'd come into her bedroom had been fuelled by anger too, the one they'd shared after she'd cried borne from an ulterior motive. Neither had been driven by genuine, heartfelt emotion. Not from him.

She did not doubt that in his quest to prove himself a better husband and prove he'd listened to her, Domenico would pull out all the stops. He would make an effort to be more affectionate and attentive. He would act the good act and treat her more like a partner than background wallpaper. She didn't doubt, either, that he would be faithful to her, and she supposed for that reason alone, he would want to have sex with her, and because she was a slave to his touch, had been until the very end of their marriage, she wouldn't resist him. He would sleep by her side rather than leave her bed as if she were some kind of doll that could be unplugged and forgotten about.

Passion, though? She could forget that. He would never allow that to happen again. Forget, too, the genuine, heartfelt emotions she'd craved throughout their marriage.

The sooner she accepted this in her heart, the better, because this was what she'd just agreed to, and it was with this in mind that she pulled a small smile to her face. 'A little.'

He returned the smile, making her heart turn over. 'Then let's go and eat.'

CHAPTER EIGHT

Domenico stepped out of the shower, dried himself off, and stood before the mirror to brush his teeth.

He was still waiting for relief at Marnie's agreement to try again to hit him. He could only assume it was her flat refusal to remarry that was stopping it from rushing out of him. The cards she'd played, although exceedingly fair, had kept them stacked in her favour. It gave not an iota of satisfaction to know she'd learned all her tricks from him.

Teeth clean, he stepped into his bedroom. His empty bedroom. His stare flicked straight to the adjoining door.

Marnie had gone to bed before him, shortly after they'd finished their dinner. Although she was recovering physically and her appetite was returning, he knew the intensity of their morning had taken its toll on her. It had taken its toll on him too. He guessed the weight of her thoughts was also playing its part.

She didn't want to try again. Not for him. Not for herself. It was all for their baby.

It shouldn't bite as much as it did.

By the time she'd gone up, her face had been drawn

with exhaustion. She'd excused herself and slipped out of the dining room without looking back at him.

Despite sharing a bedroom being part of their new agreement, it didn't surprise him that she'd retired to her own bed. Marnie needed the comfort of the familiar…

Where the hell had that thought come from?

He pushed the thought aside to be pondered another time as he instead forced himself to think of another, more probable reason she'd retired to her own room: in all their time together, he'd never invited her into his bedrooms. More than that, he'd made it very clear she wasn't welcome in them, not here in Rome or in London. He hadn't taken her to his other homes. Not after their marriage.

He reached the adjoining door with relief even further away and with a weight compressing his chest.

His perfect marriage had been made of smoke encased in the thinnest, most fragile glass, and as he recalled all Marnie had said about her reasons for marrying him, the weight grew.

It was the first time he'd properly allowed himself to think about it.

After lunch, he'd kept himself busy, first by sending out instructions for a video conference with his directors and the heads of all divisions and then having said video conference so he could personally relay the news that he would be ceasing all transatlantic travel until after the birth of his and Marnie's child. He guessed the news about the pregnancy had already spread to everyone because the surprised expressions at the news looked practised. The practicalities of his announcement had taken the rest of the afternoon to work out.

He'd been glad of it. Glad of the distraction. Glad he had something practical to get his head focused on after the intensity of all that had occurred between them in the morning. Problem-solving was something he excelled at.

He'd never expected when he married Marnie that she would be the one problem he couldn't solve.

The regularity of her breathing as he approached her bed told him she was asleep.

His heart in his throat, he slipped beneath the sheets, moving as stealthily as possible so as not to wake her.

She was curled in the foetal position with her back to him.

His eyes adjusted to the dark, Domenico stared at the back of her head and wondered what she was dreaming of. Whether or not she dreamed in sleep, she dreamed in life.

She used to dream of him rescuing her from her life, and he closed his eyes, breathing deeply to counter the ravages of his pounding heart. That's what she'd said earlier, before their baby's first movements had caught them both in their spell. He'd not been able to feel it with his hand, but he'd felt it through the joy that had lit Marnie's face, and he knew the connection that had passed between them in that moment had played a strong part in her agreement to try again. She was trying again so Domenico and their baby could forge a bond before the birth and beyond. She was pushing aside her own dreams so Domenico could live his, and as he thought this, a wave of emotion caught hold of him.

He nestled closer and gently spooned himself around her as he'd done earlier, groping for her slender hand. He wrapped his fingers around it, felt the slightest twitch in response, and pressed his mouth into her hair. She felt so damned fragile. Like she could break.

Closing his eyes, his breaths were ragged as he made a silent, fervent vow to do everything in his power to prove to Marnie that she'd made the right choice. Whatever it took, he would give her the life she used to dream of.

His last thought as he drifted into sleep was that she wasn't the one problem he couldn't solve. She was the one problem he'd been afraid to even try to solve.

Marnie's heart had ballooned before she'd pulled herself out of the twilight zone that hovered between sleep and consciousness. Her eyes pinged open, all her senses awakening in a rush.

She wasn't alone in the bed. Domenico was curved around her. His chest was pressed against her back, his arm slung over her waist, fingers curled beneath her breast, legs locked in the back of hers. As her reeling mind tried to take in that he'd joined her while she slept, she became aware of movement in the cleft of her buttocks. Her eyes widened as she felt him come to life, her thin cotton pyjama shorts giving no protection against the sensation of the growing erection nestled so perfectly that if she were naked, one hip thrust would have him inside her.

Frozen, unable to even breathe, she became aware that Domenico had stopped breathing too. The only part of her body that seemed capable of working was her heart, furiously pumping hot blood through her system, roaring in her head and pooling between her legs where the flame for him had come out of its dormant sleep at the same speed as her awakened senses. The impulse to wantonly press her buttocks tighter against him was so strong that suddenly she was breathing again, shallow inhalations through her nose as she tried desperately to keep herself like a statue and keep her focus on the armchair in her eyeline.

The curled fingers beneath her breast flickered, a light brush of the tips against her ribs. The ache inside her grew. Her breath catching back in her throat, she could do nothing about the tremor of her body as anticipation shot through her veins in an overdose of adrenaline.

The anticipated caress of her breasts never came. In one fluid motion, his hand slid off her and Domenico rolled onto his back, stretching as if he'd only that second woken.

Marnie closed her eyes, practically sagging at the weight of a disappointment she desperately wished she could deny.

Refilling her lungs as best she could, she pushed the sheets off and sat up, swinging her feet to the floor.

A hand touched her lower back. 'Good morning, *fiore mio*.'

She winced at the endearment even as his sleepy, husky voice soaked into her ears, touching her in the same way as the mark of his palm and fingers on her skin.

'Morning,' she whispered.

'You slept well?'

She nodded and cleared her throat. 'I didn't realise you'd joined me.'

'This is our new life now. One bed.' His hand caressed her back and gently gripped the side of her waist, the mattress moving as he sat up. Leaning into her, he rested his chin on her shoulder and murmured, 'Do you want to move into my room or shall I move in here?'

Sensation careering through her, she had to clear her throat again. 'Keep your room. I know you like your privacy.'

'That was then.' His cheek leaned into hers, his stubble bristling into her skin. 'This is our life now, Marnie; what we both agreed to.' He slid his hand over her waist and rested it lightly on her belly. 'You, me and our baby, unified as a family.'

Squeezing her eyes shut, she covered his hand and chanted *mindset* to herself.

She should have been better prepared for waking up with him and for him going full pelt into 'relationship mode.' This was Domenico's way. Once something was decided in his mind, he didn't waste time. He'd decided the law firm he'd inherited from his father when he was still a rookie lawyer should go international and within a decade had transformed it into one of the world's leading corporate law firms. He'd turned thirty-five and decided it was time for a child, selected Marnie as his wife and married her, all within the space of a month. Never minding his determination to have his child full-time beneath his roof; having lost her once, his pride would never allow it to happen again.

He turned his hand to thread their fingers. ‘Think about which room you would prefer to make our own, and think, too, which you would like us to share when we return to London. As for now, if you’re feeling well enough for it, what do you think about going out and taking in some of the sights Rome has to offer?’

Remembering how he’d insisted she give him the full rundown on all her sightseeing when they’d spent those months here before, she tried not to sound too flat that he’d clearly forgotten. ‘I visited them all when you brought me here last time.’

‘Those are not the sights I’m thinking about—I want to show you my past.’

She turned her cheek without thinking. The tip of her nose brushed his cheek.

He turned his face to hers and lifted his hand from her belly to brush strands of hair from her face. Thumb rubbing her cheek, his mouth only a whisper away from hers, his eyes glittered with an emotion that made her heart clutch. ‘I want to show you all the places I should have shown you the last time we were here.’

She wished her heart didn’t leap so hard at this and wished, too, that she didn’t put an automatic cynical slant on it. Domenico was starting as he meant to go on, and she needed to do the same.

Injecting some positivity into her voice, she smiled. ‘Does this mean you’re skiving off work again?’

His eyes crinkled. ‘Better than that. I’m taking the next week off.’

'Are you being serious?' In all the years Marnie had known him, the longest Domenico had taken off work had been five days over the Christmas period. That had happened only once, a few years before they'd married and only after months of nagging from his mother and sister.

He drew his head back a little and gently ran his fingers through the length of her hair. 'We need to know each other, Marnie, and we need to understand each other. It's the only way we can make it work.'

It was hard to think coherently when shivers of sensation were dancing through her skin and veins. 'I already know you, Dom.'

'I know you do, probably better than anyone, but you need to understand what underlies it all, what the drivers of my life are, just as I need to understand the drivers of your life.'

'There isn't anything to understand about me. Compared to your life and everything you've achieved, my life has been the epitome of mundanity.'

His eyes glittered. 'I don't believe that for a minute.' And then he brushed his lips to hers in a light, chaste kiss before he climbed off the bed and strolled, magnificent in his nudity, through the adjoining door.

Domenico's driver crossed the Tiber, and soon they'd driven into a bohemian neighbourhood rich with ancient buildings.

Stopping at the foot of a narrow cobbled street, their driver ignored the angry toots of other drivers while Domenico climbed out of the car and held a hand out for Marnie. To his gratification, she accepted it, only releasing his hold when she was safely on two feet.

He led her up the street, stopping when they reached a bakery with outdoor seating. He pointed across the road. 'That's the apartment I grew up in. We lived on the top two floors.'

He watched her face, the interest alive on it as she soaked in the salmon-coloured fascia.

'Do you see the balcony on the top floor? The one with all the plants?'

She nodded.

'That was my parents' bedroom. The window to the left of it was my sister's. My bedroom was at the back. My *nonna*—my grandmother—lived with us too. Her bedroom was next to mine.'

'Whose mother was she?'

'My mother's. I never knew my father's parents. My father was sixty when I was born. My *nonna* was three years younger than him.'

Marnie digested this in her usual quiet way. 'I knew he was classed as an old father, but I didn't realise he was that old.'

'There were twenty-nine years between my parents. My father and my mother's father were old friends. My father's first wife had died, and my grandparents invited him to spend Christmas with them. My mother was there. They married that summer. I was born three months later, my sister a year after that.'

'Did your father have children from his first marriage?'

'No. I believe they tried, but it didn't happen for

them.' He slipped his hand into hers and squeezed. 'Come, the offices he worked at are around the corner.'

It took a few moments for her fingers to relax in his hold, but she didn't pull them away.

Around the corner was a large piazza bustling with life. He walked with her to the ancient fountain close to the Basilica of Santa Maria and sat on its steps. 'You see that arched door?' he said, pointing at the building facing them. 'That was the door into my father's offices where he practised law. I joined the firm when I graduated and passed all my law exams under his tutelage.' He pointed to an alleyway close by. 'That, there, leads to the lower secondary school I attended. It's a hotel now, but in my years there, I would visit my father's offices on my walk home. My school finished at three, and my father insisted his diary be kept clear of appointments at that time so he was always free to greet me.'

If Domenico closed his eyes, he could hear the tap on his father's office door he always made and how he would open it without waiting for a response and step inside as his father was rising to his feet with a wide smile on his face, eyes already alive with interest at the stories his son was about to relay of his day.

'Were you very close to him?' Marnie asked softly.

He nodded, breathing out to loosen the tightness of his chest that always happened when he reminisced about his early life. 'I loved both of my parents, but always gravitated to my father. My sister always gravitated to our mother. She worked as a tour guide at the Vatican for English speakers. In our school holidays, she would often take me and my sister with her so we could absorb the English language—she was determined that we would grow up bilingual. We spoke more English in my home than Italian.'

'The Vatican's not far from here, is it?'

'About five kilometres. Easy walking distance. I walked everywhere in those days. All my family did. I never imagined I would want to live or work anywhere else.'

'So why did you?'

'A long story to be shared over a long lunch.' He stretched his neck and pointed across the piazza. 'That trattoria over there, next to that hotel, makes some of the best pasta in Rome. Shall we?'

'Sure.' She let him help her up and let him keep hold of her hand as they crossed the piazza to the trattoria that had been a staple of this district for the whole of Domenico's life.

'Was it because of your father that you chose law?' Marnie asked as they walked.

'For sure… Although there was a time when I wanted to be a professional footballer like pretty much every Italian boy grows up dreaming of being.'

She smiled. 'It was the same where I lived. All the boys wanted to be footballers.'

'And you? What did you want to be?'

She shrugged. 'I never had any career aspirations.'

Having reached the trattoria, he let that go. But only for now. 'Inside or outside?'

She tilted her face to the blue sky. 'Outside.'

The outside space being cordoned off, they settled at a corner table where fresh water was poured for them and the day's specials reeled off by the welcoming waiter.

Their orders taken, olives and breadsticks placed between them, Domenico relaxed back into his seat. Marnie's stare, he noted, was flickering all around her in every direction but at him.

He liked the dress she was wearing. The colour of autumn leaves, it was short-sleeved with a smart collar and buttons running its length. There was an unfussy simplicity to its design that perfectly suited the unfussy simplicity of the woman wearing it. But even the most seemingly simple things had hidden depths, and Marnie was one of the most potent cases of still water running deep that he'd ever known.

'So, my story for leaving Rome…'

Her stare snapped to him. Her eyes were now a deep blue. That morning, when they'd woken, they'd been a dark grey.

Dio, a man could lose himself in those eyes, whatever colour they happened to be shining.

'By the time I graduated, my father was in his eighties and getting frailer by the day. He should have retired years earlier, but he'd been looking forward to me joining him. You have to understand, he was too old to be the kind of father my friends had. He had a heart condition and was riddled with arthritis, so he couldn't play football with me or do the other physical stuff fathers do with their sons, and he felt great guilt for that. For him, us working together was the father-son thing he'd spent my life longing for, and it's to my eternal sorrow that he became too ill and frail for it to last. He held on until I qualified and became a full partner in Cannavaro Law, and then he slipped away in his sleep.'

The blue eyes widened in sympathy.

He took a deep breath. 'Two weeks after we buried him, my wife left me for my best friend.'

The wide eyes held steady. She obviously knew that part of it.

'Carmela would tell you she was a victim of my neglect. That is a way to spin it that I don't disagree with, but my neglect was never intentional, and given time, would have righted itself. I didn't set out to be a workaholic, but between my studies and my father's increased frailty, which meant I was doing as much of his work as my own, I didn't have the time to devote to her. She is very temperamental and wanted to be the centre of my world and refused to accept that my father needed me too. She punished me by having an affair with Davide.'

Her eyes clouded, compassion mingling with the sympathy. 'I'm sorry. I can't imagine anything crueller.'

'Neither could I.' He dipped a breadstick in the balsamic vinegar. 'My father's death had destroyed me. I knew it was coming, but even so…' He grimaced.

'But it was still a sucker punch,' she supplied softly. At his questioning stare, she lifted her shoulders. 'It doesn't matter if you know it's coming; nothing prepares you for losing a parent.'

The weight that seemed to have taken permanent residence in Domenico's chest pushed tighter against his ribs.

He knew Marnie's mother had died before she started working for him and that her father wasn't on the scene.

He couldn't remember how he knew about her father other than it was the kind of thing you picked up on when you spent as much time with someone as he had with her, but he knew about her mother because the first Christmas she'd worked for him he'd overheard one of the other staff asking something—he couldn't remember what—Christmas related. What he'd never forgotten was Marnie's quiet reply of, 'My mum died some time ago.'

While he'd never forgotten those words, he'd never dwelled on them either, and when six years later he'd asked about close family she wanted to invite to their wedding, he'd accepted her, 'There isn't anyone,' without pursuing it. She was such a dedicated worker that if he hadn't known she'd been born by humans, he'd have considered it perfectly plausible that Marnie was born through a cloning technique specially designed to produce the perfect assistant for him. It sat increasingly uncomfortably in him that this was how he'd seen her and treated her.

All these years, first in work and then in marriage, he'd acted as if Marnie had been put on this earth specially for him. He'd never allowed himself to think of her as fully human in her own right. As fully woman.

But she was a human, and she was all woman. A startlingly pretty woman whose beauty grew the more you looked at her, and the more he looked at her now, the harder his heart pounded painfully and guilt curdled like acid in his guts as the magnitude of his attitude towards her made itself clear to him.

This beautiful woman hadn't been beamed into his

life from a laboratory but had lived a life he'd never cared to learn about because he was a selfish, narcissistic bastard who hadn't wanted to see her as the flesh and blood woman she was. He'd been so intent on protecting his heart from further hurt that he hadn't wanted to see that Marnie had a heart that also needed protecting. And cherishing.

He would have taken her hand if steaming bowls of ravioli hadn't been brought out to them, and he took the moment to take a breath and wonder what the hell was happening to him. Something was shifting—*had* shifted—inside him, and he didn't know if it was the fact of their child growing inside her slender body… He didn't know what the hell it was, but whatever it was, it was stronger than him, and no amount of reminding himself that he'd never wanted to feel anything for her could deny the fact that he did. Just watching her spoon the soft ravioli into her mouth and chew it and swallow it and hold it down…

Dio, her suffering had marked him, and he was forced to admit he'd been more frightened he was going to lose her than he'd ever wanted to acknowledge to himself.

CHAPTER NINE

FRIGHTENED BY THE undercurrent of emotion she could see flickering on Domenico's face, frightened because she knew much of it came from his memories of his first marriage, an undercurrent of emotion she would never elicit in him, Marnie picked up the conversation. 'So was it your father's death that drove you into turning Cannavaro Law into the behemoth it is today?'

'Partly.' His eyes locked back onto hers. 'I needed to channel my grief, but I craved vengeance too; that more than anything. I wanted to make such a success of myself that Carmela spent the rest of her life regretting her treachery. My father had made modest investments in mine and my sister's names, and I taught myself to play the stock market. I studied English law and American law simultaneously and used my returns to open offices around the world. I was ruthless and focused, and everything I touched turned to gold. I hired the best lawyers to work for me—lawyers as hungry as me—and pitched for contracts I had no business pitching for and winning them, and all the while my personal fortune was exploding. Five years after Carmela left me, I was a billionaire.'

Marnie chewed slowly as she digested all that Domenico had just shared. Of course, she'd known about the wife who'd come before her, had often come close to driving herself insane with curiosity about her, and now she wished fervently that she'd put a stop to this conversation instead of driving it forward.

To build what Domenico had built out of vengeance…

His vengeance must have burned him. A flame could only blaze that bright when real emotion lay behind it.

'You must have loved her very much,' she said with as much evenness as she could manage.

'I thought I did when I married her, but in hindsight, we married because ours was a passionate lust and thought it meant we were in love.'

Something spasmed in Marnie's heart, but she calmly reached for her water and forced herself not to gulp it down.

'I wanted my father to see me settled down,' he explained. 'In my heart, I knew he didn't have much time left. Carmela and I were crazy about each other, so marriage seemed the logical thing to do.'

She had no idea how she continued to keep her voice even. 'I heard you met at school.'

'The gossips were close. We met at university, married straight after graduation and divorced three years after that.'

'It must give you great satisfaction to know your vengeance worked so well for you.'

The light brown eyes held hers. 'The man who set

out for that vengeance is a very different man to the one who married you.'

'I don't doubt it.' With a graceful smile, she got to her feet. 'Back in a mo—I need to use the ladies.'

Holding the base of her small bump, Marnie wove through the tables to the bathrooms indoors, fighting with all her might not to cry.

For the fourth morning in a row, Marnie woke to find Domenico wrapped around her. For the fourth morning in a row, she felt him waken and rouse and then roll away as if he were experiencing nothing.

Probably it was nothing to him, she thought miserably.

She only opened her eyes when she heard the bathroom door of the adjoining room close.

Rolling onto her back, she let out a deep breath and reminded herself yet again of the need for *mindset*.

She remembered hearing a song once about morning glory and asking her mother what it meant. Finding the question hugely amusing, her mother had cackled before telling her.

Morning glory. Morning erection. Apparently, if her mother was to be believed, a common denominator amongst all men.

Clearly Domenico's morning glory had nothing to do with Marnie. For the last three nights, he'd come to bed with her, stripped naked while she changed into her pyjamas in the bathroom, given her a gentle kiss goodnight and made not a single move on her, and she couldn't stop herself from questioning why.

Was it that he didn't need to bother having sex with her now that he had what he wanted? Now that she was incubating his baby?

Whatever his reasons, she supposed that at some point in the future he would want another child, and her sexual services would be required again. She supposed it might happen before then if his needs became too much for him to handle. Especially as he wouldn't be getting it anywhere else. But he was a master of self-control, so who knew. It was only Carmela who'd ignited *passionate lust* in him. The only time Marnie had ignited any passion in him had been in that awful screaming row in her flat, and it brokc her heart that it had been the passionate hate of that moment that had driven them both. The wildness of the sex itself had been glorious, but it would forever be tainted by her shameful loss of control in the build-up to it.

Marnie wished she hadn't given in to her curiosity and done an internet search of Carmela. It hadn't taken much digging to find the ex-wife of thc great Domenico Cannavaro. A few of the searches had thrown up Marnie's name, but the only picture of her was obscured, a picture from one of Domenico's many parties. She'd never been into social media or felt the need to join online business groups. Carmela, though, was a different breed. The internet was filled with an abundance of photos of her. She was jaw-droppingly beautiful, and sexy in that inimically Italian way Marnie could never come even close to achieving. No wonder Domenico had fallen into *passionate lust* with her. He wouldn't have had to be fired up with fury to have hot, passionate sex with Carmela.

She was still lying in bed brooding when he strolled back in, all showered and dressed and smelling gorgeous. He sat on the bed and leaned over her. 'How do you feel about going to a party tonight?'

'I'll check my diary and see if I'm free,' she deadpanned even as her heart thumped at the thought of getting dressed up and going out. She hadn't had a proper night out since she'd left him.

He grinned. 'Do you remember Matteo and Isla? The couple with the army of uncontrollable children?'

'She's the redhead?'

'That's the one. It's their tenth wedding anniversary, and they're throwing a party for it. Matteo heard we're in Rome and has invited us along. It should be a good night—you'll know a lot of the other faces too. Have a think about it and let me know later if you feel up to going.'

Great. Just what she wanted, to be scrutinised and gossiped about by the Italian crowd Domenico considered his real friends. Oh well, she'd committed to trying again with him. She'd have to face his friends at some point, and now that he'd mentioned a party, she found herself yearning to go.

'In that case, my diary's clear.'

His brow creased. 'You are sure? Don't agree if you think it'll take too much out of you.'

'I'm fine, Dom. I feel normal. No sickness, only a little tiredness. I'm fine.'

'Okay, but if you change your mind, don't be afraid to say.'

'I won't.'

'And when we're there—*if* we go—then as soon as you want to leave, you tell me, okay?'

'I promise.'

He pressed another of his featherlight chaste kisses that had as much meaning as the kiss from one friend to another to her mouth. 'Good.'

'What's the dress code?'

'Formal.'

She sat up. 'Then I need to go shopping for something to wear.'

His brow creased again. 'Can you manage shopping and a party in one day?'

'I'm pregnant, not an invalid.'

'I know, I just don't want you overdoing things. Why don't I get a stylist to…'

'I want to go shopping,' she interrupted firmly. 'If I'm tired when I get back, I'll have a nap.'

'When *we* get back,' he corrected before his face broke into a smile. 'I'm coming with you.'

Of course he was. Since they'd agreed to try again, he'd barely let her out of his sight. Probably afraid that the minute his back was turned, she'd change her mind and do a runner. Other than that afternoon spent video-calling all his senior staff, he'd left her alone only to take two further conference calls, which for a workaholic like Domenico was the equivalent of taking a month off, and his insistence on coming shopping with her made Marnie's stupid heart jump for joy.

While she would never admit this to him, the six months they'd spent apart had served to make her forget how quickly the hours passed when with him. Breaking away from him after all those years spent revolving her world around him had left her unmoored, as if she'd lost the gravity holding her to the here and now, and it was terrifying how quickly time was passing again and how quickly his gravity was reclaiming her.

Marnie remembered walking down *Via dei Condotti* when she'd done all her sightseeing the year before. Filled as it was with the flagship stores of most of Italy's major luxury fashion houses and high-end boutiques, she'd felt like a lost little sheep amongst Rome's elite. Rather than go into any of the stores, she'd drunk coffee in a cute little café and people-watched. She'd never, in the whole year of their marriage, been able to get her head around the fact that she was now considered one of the elite. Although she would never have fought the derisory settlement Domenico offered in their divorce, that she'd barely spent a penny of the allowance that had credited her bank account each month meant that, along with her settlement, she had a decent nest egg put aside. Obviously, it was peanuts compared to Domenico's wealth, but she'd never needed much. The last time she'd gone shopping—actual spending-money shopping—had been the day after their wedding when he'd bought half of London for her dressing room.

This shopping trip with him was a marked contrast to that last one. Or at least felt markedly different, and it wasn't just because he kept holding her hand. When she tried a dress on, he didn't just give constructive feedback with his mouth but with his eyes too. It felt like he was looking at *her*, the whole of her, Marnie, and not just a mannequin in human skin. This time, it didn't feel like she was shopping with someone treating her in the way she imagined he treated his sister on a shopping trip.

'What do you think of this?' he asked in the sixth store they entered, having shooed away the fawning sales assistants. The dress he'd pulled off the sparse rack was a seemingly simple white dress.

'It's pretty,' she said, running her fingers over the fabric. Sewn into it were thousands upon thousands of crystal sequins.

Less than a minute later, she was stripping off to her knickers in yet another luxury changing room and carefully stepping into the white dress. Backless, she was able to do the hidden zip up herself as it only ran to the base of her spine, and then she pulled it over her breasts, securing them in the inbuilt bra, and tied the halter-neck straps around her neck, being careful not to catch her hair in it.

Only then did she allow herself to look at her reflection.

Her chest expanded. The dress was beautiful. By going up a size to what she normally wore, it accommodated her growing belly and breasts—she hadn't paid much attention to them growing too—without constricting them, giving her an hourglass figure. The top part of it skimmed her cleavage in a circle, and as the halter-neck straps were gold, it gave the illusion of the dress defying gravity. When she turned this way and that, the crystal sequins caught the light and sparkled a rainbow of colours.

And then her chest deflated. She was much too plain to wear this. Wearing it made her feel like a mutton pretending to be a lamb.

Just as she was determining to change out of it, there was a knock on the dressing room door followed by Domenico's voice. 'Are you okay in there?'

Injecting some lightness into her voice, she called back, 'I'm fine. Just took a while to get into the dress.'

'Are you going to let me see?'

'No point. It isn't right for me.'

There was something in the way Marnie said *it isn't right for me* that made Domenico pause. Wistful. That's how she sounded.

So far, she'd tried on eight dresses. To his eyes, she'd looked beautiful in all of them, but he'd understood her objections. Growing up with a fashion-conscious mother and sister had made him aware of the necessity for a woman to not just look good in an outfit but to feel good in it. Marnie's *it isn't right for me* didn't sound like one of the usual objections of a dress being too long or too short or too old or too young for her.

'Can I see anyway?' he asked steadily.

The answer came via the door unlocking. She pulled it open and stepped back with the same wistful expression on her face as had been in her voice.

Domenico's heart rose and caught in his throat, and it took a long moment before he could clear it enough to say, 'Marnie, this dress looks beautiful on you.'

Colour slashed her cheeks, and she rubbed her arms. 'I love the dress, but…' She shook her head, the colour on her face darkening even more. 'It's too sparkly. It needs to be worn by someone beautiful and vivacious who can carry it off.'

Dumbfounded that she could say that and, worse, mean it, it took another long moment before he spurred himself into action. Stepping into the dressing room, he closed the door. 'Turn around.'

Her eyebrows drew together in question.

Gently gripping her shoulders, he manoeuvred her until she was facing the mirror and stood behind her.

Putting his hands on her hips, he looked over her head to catch her stare in the mirror's reflection. 'Do you know what I see?'

Her eyebrows drew together again.

'I see a vision of beauty.' He wrapped his arms around her waist and rested his chin on the top of her head. She was wearing perfume, and it had mingled with her shampoo to create a scent so divine it was all he could do to stop himself burying his face in her neck and greedily inhaling it deep into her lungs. Holding her like this was the most he could allow himself. The most he dared. 'The dress sparkles, but you, *fiore mio*, dazzle in it. This dress was made for you, and I don't understand why you can't see it.'

After a long beat, her shoulders rose before she sighed and leaned back into him. Quietly, she said, 'I just see me.'

'Then the me you see is different to the me I see. You're beautiful, Marnie, and you deserve to sparkle.' Soon, he was determined to understand why she couldn't see it.

Her eyes glistened, sparkling as much as her dress, but she delicately sniffed the tears back before they could fall. 'You think I should get it?'

He shook his head. 'I *know* you should get it.'

More aware than he'd been when he entered the room of the intimacy of its confines and with the heat of Marnie's body and her scent all swirling inside him to heat the arousal he was determined to keep under lock and key while she was so fragile, Domenico knew it was time to leave the room. It was bad enough that he was already torturing himself with his need to hold her the whole night through…holding her without touching her. Keeping her at a distance that was the opposite of the distance he'd put her through during their marriage. This physical distance… *Dio*, he mustn't think about it. While Marnie was still recovering from those months of illness, he must keep his desire controlled. She was too fragile.

But he could allow his hands to stroke the length of her bare arms, and he could drop a kiss into the irresistible arch of her neck… *Dio*, how had he been so blind for all those years?

His blindness had been wilful. That was becoming clearer by the day. By the minute. Blind not only to Marnie's luminescent beauty but to his feelings for her. Too blind to notice she'd slipped beneath the wall he'd built in the wake of his father's death and the breakdown of his first marriage…

Clearing his throat, he stepped away from her. 'I will leave you to change.'

Her eye caught his again in the mirror's reflection. Her hand rose to her throat. She lifted her chin and nodded.

Feeling as if his heart was trying to punch its way out of his ribs, Domenico closed the door behind him.

The party itself was everything Marnie had expected. Held in the grounds of Matteo and Isla's magnificent two-storey apartment, barely a five-minute walk from the boutique she'd chosen her dress in, it was filled with more faces that were familiar than unfamiliar.

When Domenico had thrown his parties when she'd been his PA and expected to attend them in that still undefined supervisory capacity, she'd hidden behind her job title, using it as a mask to conceal how intimidated she felt amongst all his glamorous and successful friends. When she was his wife, she'd been pushed forward, into the throng of the glamorous and successful friends, and it had been excruciating for her. She'd wanted to cling to Domenico's coattails the way she'd done since she was eighteen, but this time for real rather than as a metaphorical thing. Who was she, she'd always fretted, no matter how kindly she was treated, to even think of standing tall amongst these people?

This time, it had all changed again. She didn't know if it was the genuine warmth she found in his friends' eyes or the tightness of the embraces she was given, or the genuine gushes of congratulations about them and the baby, or even if it was the beautiful dress she was wearing, but she didn't feel the need to hide behind Domenico, nor cringe inwardly when approached by anyone. She felt different in herself. Stronger.

The biggest change was in how Domenico was with her. He'd been attentive and solicitous since their agreement to try again, but this was their first time together in their new incarnation out in society. The changes were subtle, but it was the impact they had on Marnie that made them feel so big.

Parties during their marriage had been spent not just trying to be invisible but feeling invisible to Domenico. It wasn't that he'd left her to fend for herself, more that he'd never felt the need to draw her into conversations, had been content for her to hang by his side like a forgotten appendage. Tonight, he pulled her to the fore, keeping her hand firmly in his or an arm around her waist, making sure she was included in everything, translating when needed, and always ensuring she had a glass of water to sip on. And when she caught his eye…

It no longer felt like it used to, like he was looking through her. When Domenico looked at her now, it felt like he was seeing the whole of her. There were even times when their eyes locked, and the longing she just could not shake for him seemed to be mirrored in his stare. She thought she'd seen that longing in the changing room earlier, that spellbinding moment when it felt like all the air had been sucked out of the room. That little kiss he'd placed on her neck…she could still feel the mark of his lips on her skin. Still feel the flush of heat that had followed it.

She'd experienced another, deeper, flush of heat when she'd left her dressing room and found him waiting for her on the bedroom sofa. She could spend a thousand years with Domenico and never become inured to his masculine beauty, but there were times when she looked at him and the effect was like a bolt of lightning straight into her heart. Tonight had been one such time, and when their eyes had finally fused and she'd seen the pulse resonating from his…

For the first time in her life, Marnie had felt not just beautiful but desirable. The bolt in her heart had spread in a flush of heat so strong that it had taken all her strength not to throw herself into his arms.

'How are you feeling?' he murmured into her ear when the group they'd been talking to headed onto the makeshift dance floor.

It seemed like everyone was now on the dance floor, even the hosts' tearaway children, who'd snuck out of their bedrooms and had been spotted minesweeping the empty glasses. Marnie remembered doing that once, as a small child. Her dad had still been there then. She'd got out of bed early and found an empty bottle of alcohol she now knew was vodka and two glasses on the coffee table. One of the glasses had still been half full. She'd drunk it all and then spent the day vomiting and feeling wretched. It had taken two decades for her to get even a little bit drunk again. That had been the day their decree nisi had come through.

It had been the first time since she'd left him that she'd been unable to ignore the depth of her misery without him. All the pretence she'd shrouded herself in had stripped away, and suddenly it hadn't mattered that leaving him had been a necessity, not when the pain of living without him had become so terrifyingly acute. And so she'd bought that bottle of wine, fully understanding for the first time why her mother had sought consolation in the bottom of a bottle, and for the first time allowed herself to rage and grieve at the loss of her dreams and the loss of the man she'd built her world around.

And then he'd knocked on her door, and the child growing safely in her belly had been conceived.

Was it possible, she asked herself for the first time, that Domenico had come to her that night because he'd been experiencing similar feelings…? Had he felt her loss like she'd felt his…?

Her heart suddenly thumping hard, she lifted her gaze to his. He was still looking at her. Still looking at her as if she meant something to him.

Was it really possible, she wondered dazedly. Being invisible and forgettable was so deeply ingrained that she'd never considered the possibility of Domenico missing her and…dare she even think it…? developing feelings for her…

Close to choking on emotion, she had to swallow to truthfully say, 'I'm feeling better than I have in a long time.'

Sensuous lips curving, he gently traced the rim of her ear. 'You're enjoying yourself?'

Shivers of sensation danced through her, and she squeezed the fingers entwined through hers and nodded. 'Can we dance?'

The words had come out before she knew she was going to say them, but the longing that accompanied them was as impossible to deny as her longing for him. They'd danced together only once, at their wedding reception. It had been a token dance to an upbeat song. She'd watched Domenico dance at his parties many times before they married, but other than that token dance, never while they were married. He'd avoided the dance floor until she'd left him.

Why was that? Why had he been so reluctant to take her into his arms for a simple dance? Had it even *been* reluctance? And why had she never asked *him* to dance? Why had she been so content to let him take the lead on every single aspect of their marriage?

As all these thoughts and questions flew through her head, his jaw clenched and flexed, and his eyes briefly closed before fixing back on hers. With a tug of his hand, he led her through the dancing bodies to the last available space on the floor and stiffly drew her to him.

CHAPTER TEN

DOMENICO'S HEART WAS beating impossibly hard. All evening, he'd worked hard to block out the effect Marnie was having on him. It was an effect he'd been trying to block since he'd left her in the boutique's changing room, and now, with only his shirt separating her warm cheek from his chest and the softness of her blond hair brushing beneath his chin, it was taking all his control not to squeeze her tightly to him.

She just felt so damned good to hold. Smelt so damned good, too. Better than good. Holding her in his arms at night was torturous, but to feel her hot body swaying against his, the crush of her breasts, the gentle curve of her hips, to know one movement of his leg would lock their groins together…

He clenched his teeth even as he gave into temptation and palmed his hand up the length of her naked back and dove his fingers into her long hair. It all felt like the finest silk.

He could hardly breathe. The hot, thick desire that had been a constant battle to suppress these last few days was unfurling at a speed he couldn't control, and when Marnie lifted her face and her wide eyes locked on his, he knew she'd felt the ridge of his arousal against her abdomen. It was impossible to ascertain their colour. He could only see the pulse he knew must be mirrored in his own stare.

Domenico sustained the torture for three more tracks, until a commotion caused by the hosts' unruly children being frogmarched back to their rooms provided a natural break, and he released his hold around her and finally took in a breath of air that wasn't laced with her heady perfume.

The rest of the night passed in a blur, Domenico torn between aching for Marnie to tell him she was ready to call it a night and praying for her not to.

He had to get a grip on himself. Making love to her was out of the question, even if he was finding it impossible to stop himself from touching her, a need that had nothing to do with proving his newfound attentiveness. He could barely comprehend the depth of his need to just *touch* her, never mind all the other impossible feelings coursing through him, and for the first time he was forced to acknowledge it wasn't just fear of hurting her fragile body that was holding him back from making love to her. All these hot, heady feelings… *Dio*, his need for her.

He'd needed her that night. Anger and wounded pride hadn't been the only driving forces taking him to her. He'd needed her. Needed to just *see* her, and then all those feelings had exploded, and it had turned into the most incredible night of his life.

Dio, his feelings for her were a hot mess and growing messier by the second. And stronger. It felt like he was clinging on by his fingertips without knowing what he was clinging on *to*.

The internal fight continued on the drive home. Bodies only inches apart, fingers laced tightly together, the only sound in their cocoon was the roar of blood whooshing in Domenico's ears, his thoughts all coalesced around how the hell he was going to climb beneath the bed sheets with her and keep his damned hands to himself.

He would keep his damned hands to himself by turning himself into stone. It was the only way. Envisage himself as being made of granite. No. Diamond. Diamonds were impermeable.

Closing the door to her bedroom, he turned his thoughts into diamonds as well, but when he looked at her, he was unable to blur her beautiful face.

Dio, she was so damned ravishing. The ache to breach the distance between them…

He snapped his stare away from her. 'I'm going to have a nightcap downstairs,' he said shortly, unable to temper the roughness in his voice. 'I'm sure you'll be asleep when I come back up, so I'll wish you a good night now. Sleep well, *cuoricina*.'

He'd barely uttered the last of his endearment before he'd closed the door behind him.

Marnie stared at the bedroom door in a form of shell shock at Domenico's abrupt departure. He hadn't even given her the usual cursory goodnight kiss.

The heart that had been beating with anticipation the whole drive home had now squeezed into a tight ball that was almost impossible to breathe through. His rejection…

Their whole marriage had been one long, barely subtle rejection. It had never wounded as deeply as this.

Feeling like she could be sick, she unzipped her dress and untied the gold halter neck. Her beautiful dress fell to her feet. She stepped out of it without looking down. She couldn't bear to see it, not when she'd felt sick with the anticipation of Domenico stripping it from her. The desirable beauty she'd imagined herself to be in his eyes had been nothing but a fantasy.

When would she learn? He didn't want her; he wanted their baby. All his affection and attention were just performance.

But it hadn't felt like a performance. Not the look in his eyes or the way he'd held her on the dance floor. Nor the arousal she'd felt as a ridge against her belly. It had all felt so real. Felt like her long-ago dream was blossoming into life.

A flare of anger, not at Domenico but at herself, cut through her misery. Wasn't this what she'd done before? Let herself be caught up in a fantasy that had no basis in reality?

But the way he'd caressed her naked back on the dance floor had felt real…

Stop it, she furiously admonished herself. Near tears with all the emotions fighting inside of her, she practically threw herself into the shower. If she could wash away his touch from her skin, she'd feel better, she was certain of it.

Her certainty wasn't worth the paper it was written on.

Naked, her body clean, her face stripped of the makeup she'd adorned it with for the party, she gazed at her ordinary, plain reflection and blinked back more tears. Any beauty she'd possessed that evening had been illusory.

She'd been chosen by Domenico for her plainness and docility. He'd experienced hot lust and passion with the vibrant, beautiful Carmela and been burned for it. Marnie, the wallflower forgotten by her father and barely acknowledged by her mother, was the antithesis of the sexy Italian woman. He'd married her because she posed zero threat to his equilibrium.

Oh, *why* had he held her the way he had on the dance floor? Why had he looked at her the way he had the whole evening? She hadn't imagined it, she *hadn't*, so why would he put on an act like that when he didn't need to?

Fearing her brain could explode from all her despairing thoughts, Marnie shrugged her arms into her robe and tied the sash, and then, barely conscious of what she was doing, walked out of the bathroom and through the bedroom and out of the door.

With Domenico's admonition of her always bottling her unhappiness ringing in her ears, she padded down the stairs in search of him. By the time she found him, her heart was as ready to explode as her brain was.

He was in the main living room, his feet up, half-reclined on the reclining armchair, his shirt unbuttoned at the throat. An empty crystal glass in his hand, he was watching a game of football with the sound off. At least, she thought he was watching it. There was something distant in his expression that made her feel that whatever was happening on the screen wasn't penetrating any deeper than the membrane of his eyes, and there was something about the distance of his expression that made her heart catch in her throat. When her presence in the far corner of the room finally caught his attention, his head jerked, and he blinked as if disbelieving of what his eyes were telling him. And then his face slipped into the same mask it had worn when he'd wished her a good night.

'Is something wrong, Marnie?' he asked steadily.

It took all her courage to force her feet across the floor.

By the time she reached him, her legs were shaking so hard that she perched herself on the sofa facing him.

Her heart thrashing, she managed only a shallow breath before finding the courage to say, 'Why don't you want to make love to me?'

Something spasmed over his gorgeous face, but then he moved his stare away from her. His voice, when he finally answered, remained steady. 'Of course I want to make love to you.'

'Do you?'

His jaw tightening, the knuckles of the fingers holding his glass whitening, he inclined his head.

Her heart wrenched, blood rushing to her head at the sudden certainty that he was lying. 'Then why do you keep rejecting me?'

He hung his head and grabbed his skull with his free hand. 'Marnie…'

She'd shot to her feet before her brain knew what she was doing, and fumbled with the sash of her robe. 'Look at me, Dom. Look at me and tell me what's so wrong with me that you can't bring yourself to make love to me. Look at me and tell me why you want me to commit the rest of my life to you when you don't want *me*.'

Only because he could no longer deny Marnie anything did Domenico lift his stare to her.

Dio del Cielo. She'd opened her robe. He'd known from the way her breasts had moved when she'd walked across the room that she was naked, but to have it proved right when she stood only feet away from him…

'How can you doubt that I want you?' he asked hoarsely, only just managing to successfully blur his eyes to her nakedness. All his efforts to turn himself back into a diamond were collapsing around him. 'Now, please, close your robe.' He swallowed the moisture that had filled his mouth and tried to blur his brain from the searing image of her beautiful naked body. 'I—'

'I said *look* at me,' she cried, slipping the robe off and stepping towards him. 'You've been with hundreds of women of all different shapes and sizes, so tell me what's so wrong with me that the only way you can bring yourself to make love to me is when you want to make a baby or when you're drunk.'

He'd kicked his recliner seat upright, slammed his

glass on the table to the side of his chair and grabbed hold of her hips before he could stop himself.

He forced himself to unblur his eyes and meet her stare. There was such distress in it that something inside of him broke. His fingers losing the grip they'd been clinging to, he plunged head first into the truth of his feelings for her.

'I do want to make love to you, Marnie,' he whispered raggedly, 'more than I have ever wanted anything, but you're so fragile that I don't want to do anything that could hurt you.'

Her eyes…they were a stormy grey…widened, her breath audibly catching in her throat.

He skimmed a trembling hand over her breasts. Pregnancy had made them swell like it was making her stomach swell, and all he could think was that she was the Venus de Milo come to life, but a million times more beautiful.

Pulling her closer, he wrapped his arms around her and pressed his cheek to the soft, succulent breasts. He could hear the rapid thump of her heart beneath his ear, a sound that filled him with so much emotion that if he could burrow his hand through her skin and hold it in his hands, he would. He would hold it and cherish it, do all the things he should have done when they were married.

'I want you so badly it hurts,' he confessed. 'Tonight… I didn't reject you, *fiore mio*, never think that, but you're so small and I'm so big and bulky that I fear I will break you. I think of all you have suffered carrying our child, and I will wait however long it takes before I make love to you again because all that matters to me is that you are here with me, back in my life where you belong.'

Just as he belonged to her.

If it wasn't for the thud of her heart against his ear, he'd fear Marnie had turned to the stone he'd tried to turn himself into. She didn't move a muscle.

Then, after time seemed to have stretched to the end of eternity, her fingers slipped tentatively through his hair.

Domenico expelled his first proper breath since she'd walked into the room and nuzzled his cheek tighter into her. The fingers of her other hand joined the first, clasping his skull and tilting his head back.

He opened his eyes. The storm of the grey in her stare had disappeared, but there was no calmness in it. The storm had been replaced with an emotion so potent he felt it penetrate every cell of his body.

She leaned her beautiful face to his, close enough that he could feel her breath on his face, and whispered, 'You can't break me, Dom.'

Her scent swirling through his senses, he clenched his hands into fists, barely able to speak for the desire thrumming so wildly inside him. 'I don't want to hurt you.' Not in any way. Never again.

'Then you won't.' With a boldness Marnie had never dreamed she possessed, she cupped Domenico's cheeks and pressed her mouth to his, holding it there as she breathed his dark taste deep into her lungs.

He *did* want her. Wanted her with the same depth of need that she wanted him. She'd seen it in his eyes, heard it in his voice, and now she could feel it in the tremors of his magnificent body as he continued to resist the desire that belonged to them both.

Belonged to them both.

Maybe he would never have the great passionate lust for Marnie that he'd once felt for Carmela, but he did want her. He desired her. Felt enough for her that he would put his own needs aside for her protection. That meant something. It might not be the something she'd once so desperately craved, but it was enough.

She didn't want protecting. Not anymore. She just wanted him, the man who'd captured her heart when she'd been only eighteen years old.

Moving her mouth slowly against his, she slid her fingers back into his hair, threading the soft strands in the way she'd ached to do when they were married. And, slowly, he responded. Slowly, the taut lips relaxed and began to move with hers. Slowly, the fists behind her back loosened, his hands spreading open and flattening tightly against her skin.

With a shuddering breath, he moved his mouth away and pressed his forehead to hers. 'Are you sure about this?'

She gazed into the gorgeous eyes pulsing with his hunger for her. 'More certain than I've ever been about anything.'

A bone-deep certainty that wasn't fuelled by unrealistic dreams. The Marnie who'd married with those unrealistic dreams didn't exist anymore. She didn't doubt that Domenico could still hurt her emotionally—that had already been proved that night—but how she reacted to it was in her own hands. He could only hurt her if she let him.

His eyes closed, the strong column of his throat moved, and then he was sliding a hand beneath her bottom and rising to his feet, lifting her with him until she was nestled securely in his arms. Without another word spoken, he carried her out of the room and up the stairs.

It was beyond magical to be carried in Domenico's arms in the way she'd once dreamed he would do on their wedding night, and when he kicked open the bedroom door, her heart ballooned so big it threatened to choke her.

He'd kicked open the door to his room.

Since she'd agreed to try again, they'd only shared her bed. Although Domenico had said she could choose which of their two rooms to make their own, she'd not set foot into his territory, and he'd extended no invitation for her to enter it.

That he was carrying her across the threshold of his room signified the crossing of a much more significant threshold, and it was all she could do to snatch air through the suffocating emotion in her chest.

Feeling like he had the most precious cargo in the world in his arms, Domenico gently laid Marnie on the turned-down bed.

Needing a moment to gather himself, he sat beside her and soaked her in. The staff had switched on the headboard lights. They cast her in a perfect soft, golden glow.

He'd never allowed himself to look at her naked before. Not truly look at her. He'd never allowed himself to see the smooth perfection of her lightly golden skin or the plumpness of her milky breasts and the perfect roundness of her pale pink nipples.

His heart thumped harder as his gaze drifted lower, over the swell of the belly that used to be flat, down to the neat pubic mound. The dark blond hair there was as soft as the hair on her head, he remembered. He'd stroked that hair more times than he could ever count, but never the long blond locks of her head. It had been an intimacy he'd refused to allow in his desperate quest to keep his wife at a distance.

During their marriage, he'd always gone to her bed when she was already tucked beneath the sheets. He'd always made love to her with the lights out.

No, he acknowledged painfully. He hadn't made love to her. He'd never allowed that. He'd never allowed true intimacy, only sexual intimacy. Even that sexual intimacy had come with barriers.

Was it any wonder she'd become so desperately unhappy, he thought wretchedly. The one night the barriers he'd erected had broken, it had been anger driving them both in their wild coupling. Anger and misery and despair.

Marnie had been desperately unhappy with him. Domenico had been desperately unhappy without her. He'd just been too arrogant, stubborn and pigheaded to realise either of their unhappiness.

Too blind to realise he'd been in love with her all along…

It felt like a hammer slammed against his ribs,

and suddenly he could feel the scald of heat crawling through him as the truth he'd plunged into when his fingers had lost their grip hit him even harder.

He loved her. Loved Marnie. Loved her with every fibre of his being.

Rubbing his thumb over her flushed, high cheekbone, he breathed a gentle kiss to the softest lips on this earth and breathed in the softness of her clean skin. When he drew back, her eyes were liquid.

CHAPTER ELEVEN

Domenico undressed slowly, keeping his eyes fixed on Marnie's as he unbuttoned his shirt and unzipped his trousers. He experienced only fleeting relief when he freed his arousal from the confines of his underwear.

Not a word was exchanged. Not a word was needed. Their locked eyes did all the talking for them.

Naked, he stretched out beside her and propped himself on an elbow to gaze down at her. His chest felt so full with his love for her that anything but shallow breaths was impossible.

Closing his eyes, he brought his face down to hers to capture her mouth in a lingering, featherlight kiss. And then he kissed her again.

Slowly, their lips fused and began to move. Delicate fingers reached into his hair as their lips parted. The tips of their tongues flicked together, electrifying him with sensation.

Mouths and tongues entwined; the kiss deepened.

If the kiss they'd shared after their child had moved had been the kiss of Marnie's dreams, then this was the kiss of her life. With the glorious taste and scent of Domenico filling her senses, she slipped away from the world. Her lips and tongue didn't just follow his lead but made demands of their own, kissing and being kissed with such passion that she wanted to cry from the emotion of it all, and she moaned into his mouth at the exquisite sensation of his finger circling her ear and trailing down her neck…

Oh, but it was nothing on the sensation that filled her when his fingers skimmed to her breasts and he cupped one in his palm. Caressingly, he kneaded the sensitive flesh, and when he ran his thumb over her hardened nipple, a bolt of sensation flew directly to the flame burning in her pelvis.

His mouth moving away from hers, he draped a thigh between her legs, and then his lips were following the trail made by his fingers.

The shock of pleasure when he took a breast whole in his mouth and sucked was so acute that she cried out, the cry deepening into low, throaty moans as he slowly encircled her hardened peaks with languorous strokes of his tongue and teasing bites of his teeth. Oh, but this was *heavenly*…

While his mouth continued pleasuring her breasts, his hand roamed her body in a tender, unhurried exploration, as if he were touching her for the very first time.

It felt like he *was* touching her for the very first time.

Her fingers burrowed in his hair, Marnie closed her eyes and sank into the thrills cascading through her.

How, Domenico wondered dimly as his teeth gently bit the underside of Marnie's breast, had he never before acknowledged the soft perfection of her skin? The soft perfection of *her*?

Dio del Cielo, how had he closed himself off so fully that his reaction to her virginity had been to want to slam a door on their marriage?

He'd made it good for her, he knew that, but he'd deliberately done the bare basics. Selfish, selfish bastard.

Dio, he would give anything to turn back time and do that night again. Do their marriage again. Rewind even further, back to their proposal. Get down on one knee and promise to love and cherish her forever.

Snaking his way down the belly in which their child was safely thriving, he kissed every inch of her flesh, a need even stronger than the arousal burning through him to make this the night he should have given her on their wedding night.

His arrogance in thinking *he'd* been the catch when all along this soft, gentle woman had been loving him and wanting only his love in return.

Marnie had given her body and heart to him, and he'd used her body and trampled on her heart.

He could never take back what he'd done, but he would do his damnedest to make it up to her and worship her as he should always have done.

Dipping his tongue into her navel, Domenico kissed his way down to her pubis, an act he'd only performed the night they'd conceived their child.

Dio, she smelt so damned good, and anticipation throbbed to know he was about to taste her again.

As he lay flat on the bed between her trembling legs and gently clasped her thighs to raise and part them, he dimly wondered for the first time if he'd resisted this particular intimacy for the whole of their marriage *because* he'd known the effect it would have on him. How many times had his nostrils twitched when she'd passed him in the office at the divine scent that followed in her wake…?

Inhaling the divine scent of her sex deep into his lungs, he groaned to find her already swollen.

She'd always been so damned responsive to him.

And he'd always been so damned responsive to her. More responsive than he'd ever wanted to be.

He was done hiding and fighting. Marnie deserved the world. Tonight, he would give it to her. He would give her the love he'd always denied her. Denied them both.

Closing his eyes, he dipped lower and probed his tongue right in the heart of her femininity. With barely tempered darts of his tongue, he explored her most intimate, secret flesh, thrilling at her soft moans of pleasure, soft moans that deepened when he danced his tongue back up to the swollen pulse.

Marnie's eyes flew open at the dose of untrammelled pleasure that had just shot through her, and suddenly she couldn't breathe for the anticipation of what he was about to do to her and the pleasure that would be unleashed. Her flesh was on fire, her blood lava, the heat stoking her coming not just from the wonderous things Domenico was doing to her but the *way* he was doing them. The emotion driving them.

Oh, God, she wanted to cry again from the beauty of it all, but then there were no more thoughts of tears because his tongue pressed against her nub again and stayed there, and in the beat of a heart, Marnie had tumbled head first into a world of the most heavenly sensation.

As the pressure of Domenico's tongue slowly increased, Marnie lost all sense of herself. She had no sense of the moans coming from her mouth or awareness of her back and neck arching as she writhed into him. She was chasing the pleasure, and then she was riding it, riding the waves taking her higher and higher until she reached the crescendo and shattered into a kaleidoscope of pulsating ecstasy.

Time slipped away as she slowly floated back down to a world that contained only Domenico.

She opened her eyes and locked gazes with him. Her heart was racing so hard she couldn't feel the individual beats.

He lifted himself up and carefully enveloped her with his body.

Their eyes locked back together. She palmed his cheek. Her heart felt fit for bursting to see the emotion emanating from his stare. Oh, but it felt like she'd waited her whole life to see that. Felt like she'd waited her whole life for this.

Jaw tightening, nostrils flaring, he lowered his head and fused his mouth to hers.

Fresh sensation bloomed into life.

Domenico had never felt anything close to what he was feeling now. Hot blood was pumping relentlessly through him, his arousal a fever burning through his veins. *Dio*, the way Marnie had come apart for him…

He'd never experienced anything like it, not in the

whole of his life, and now, with her tongue entwined with his and her nails scratching through his hair…

Ti prego Dio, don't let me hurt her.

Breaking the kiss, perspiration broke out on his skin as he lifted what little of his weight he had on her so only the tips of her breasts were brushed against his chest. He reached down to grip hold of his erection.

Don't let me hurt her.

Eyes locked together, he guided his arousal to her opening and kept tight hold of it as he slowly inched his way inside her.

Mio Dio, he could feel *everything.*

He drove a little further into the tightness of her velvet heat. He could feel the lids of his eyes getting heavy, his features tightening, his breaths deepening, but he refused to break the fuse of their stares, not even when he finally released his hold on his erection and rested his forearms either side of her and used his hips to drive the last few inches of his length inside her.

Their groins locked together. He had no control of the shudder his body made at the sensations pulsating through him.

Mio Dio…

Swallowing hard to keep himself in check, Domenico could hardly open his throat to drag out, 'Are you okay?'

It was all Marnie could do to move her head in assent. She was incapable of speaking. She could feel every inch of his length tight inside her. He wasn't just filling her; he was a part of her in a way she had never felt before. And she could feel his restraint, too, not just see it in the tautness of his jaw and the hardness shining in the molten of his eyes. Her pounding heart melted for him, thrills of an intensity she'd never felt before uncoiling inside her, and, suddenly desperate to get even closer to him, she wrapped her legs around his waist and lifted her head to kiss him.

He groaned into her mouth, the groan deepening when she dragged her fingers down the long length of his muscular back and groped his tight buttock.

'Marnie…'

She broke his hoarse protest with another kiss before palming his cheek. Gazing deep into the hooded, molten eyes, she whispered, 'Make me yours, Domenico.'

After a long, spellbinding moment, he breathed deeply and then, with an expression of the utmost pain, he began to move. His thrusts were short and tempered, the lock of their groins never breaking, but even as sensation built back up and began to saturate her and the flame in her pelvis stoked back into a furnace, all she could see was his gorgeous features taut with concentration.

Her heart melting all over again for him, Marie lifted her head for another kiss, and as their lips locked together, she tilted her hips.

His groan was barely perceptible.

Lips fastened, she wrapped her limbs tightly around him and closed her eyes.

Slowly, the rhythm of their lovemaking began to change. The tempered restraint slipped away as the strokes inside her lengthened and deepened. His cheek tight against hers, his breath hot on her skin, the groans coming from his throat became more ragged and drawn, and then a hand was reaching for hers, fingers entwining, every inch of them fusing together in a sensation that had white light flickering behind her eyes.

She'd never known such pleasure existed, and when her climax came, she buried her face in his neck and held him tightly, spasming as pulsating flames of bliss rippled through her entire being like an inferno.

Somehow, Domenico's throaty groans deepened further, and then he was driving himself so deeply inside her that another climax rippled through her. As the rapture recaptured her, the beautiful body making such glorious love to her went rigid, and the fingers laced with hers tightened, and when he finally let go, it was with a hoarse cry of her name.

Domenico held Marnie close to him. They were nestled together, legs entwined, her cheek resting in the crook of his shoulder.

His heart was still racing. He still couldn't breathe properly. He could barely gather his thoughts.

He'd never lain after making love feeling like this before. Only one night had come close to it. The night he and Marnie had conceived their child.

He'd let her kick him out the next morning without a fight because everything he'd felt that night and everything he'd felt when he'd woken had been too much. Everything he'd felt then and everything he was feeling now was everything he'd spent their marriage fighting, and all because he'd been afraid. Afraid of letting her get too close, afraid of making love with more than his body, and all because he'd been afraid of feeling like this. All that fight and all that fear, never realising it was too late. It had always been too late. The fight to preserve his heart had been lost long ago.

He swallowed air into his lungs and pushed it out through his nose. Finally, he was able to ask, 'Are you okay?'

The arm around him tightened in assent.

He pressed his mouth to the top of her head and held it there. The memories of what they'd just shared floated before him.

But even as his mind and heart raced at the beauty of what they'd shared, guilt sharpened in his guts that he'd never allowed it to be like that for them before.

The hand gently stroking his back slipped away and gripped his forearm, tugging it to make it move. Wordlessly, she brushed down to take hold of his hand and guided it to her belly. 'Press there,' she whispered.

Closing his eyes, he pressed his flattened hand as hard as he dared to the small bump.

After a long time had passed, she quietly asked, 'Can you feel it?'

He shook his head and kissed her forehead.

She tilted her head to capture his stare and smiled ruefully. 'The flutters felt a little stronger than last time.'

He leaned his face down to kiss her mouth. 'It will happen soon,' he promised.

Palming his cheek, she sighed and moved her body even tighter against his and extended her neck in search of another kiss.

* * *

There was something incredibly romantic about sharing a bath, Marnie thought dreamily. Especially when it was a sunken bath in a bathroom that wouldn't have looked out of place in ancient Rome. And especially when you were leaning back against a man as dreamily gorgeous as Domenico with your cheek pressed tight against his, and one of his hands was kneading your breasts, the other dipped between your legs, masturbating you to a climax.

She felt no inhibitions in moaning her pleasure. On the contrary. She felt free. As light as a bird. And, just like a bird, she was soaring as Domenico's pleasuring fingers worked their magic, and when she came, it was with an unrestrained cry that had barely echoed away when he lifted her by the hips and then pulled her back down to sink onto his hard length. His mouth hot on the side of her neck, he held her securely as he thrust up into her with rapid strokes that brought him to his own rapid climax with an unrestrained cry of his own.

Only when she felt the tension of his orgasm loosen did she laugh and turn her face to kiss him. Grinning, he returned the kiss before lifting her enough to slide his deflating erection out of her.

Once she'd resettled back between his legs, he gave a contented sigh and wrapped his arms back around her…back around her because that's how they'd started.

With the solid comfort of Domenico's body behind her, his arms covering her stomach and the warmth of the bathwater cocooning her, Marnie closed her eyes. She felt like she could finally fall asleep. She'd come close a few times, but a switch in her brain had refused to turn off.

Her dream had finally come true. It had come better than true. The man she'd worshipped for the whole of her adult life had made love to her, not through furious, pride-induced anger but through genuine, heartfelt emotion. Falling asleep meant waking back to reality, and she hadn't been ready for that. Not when she didn't know what the reality of tomorrow would look like.

Maybe it had been the same for Domenico because he'd shown no sign of wanting to fall asleep either. Instead, they'd made love again, and then again. And still neither had fallen asleep, but by the time he'd lazily suggested a bath, the reality of what tomorrow would bring no longer frightened her. It was already tomorrow. The sun would soon be rising, and the birds she felt as free and as light as would awaken.

'Tell me something,' he said softly, breaking through her contented thoughts.

She stretched her legs and stroked his arms. 'What do you want to know?'

'Why you didn't fight me over the settlement. It wouldn't have taken much fight. I offered it out of spite, you must have known that. And you must have known I never expected you to agree to it.'

'I wanted a clean break, and besides, your money belongs to you, not me. You earned it.'

'But you were my wife and entitled to a decent settlement, and you knew that too. You didn't have to be greedy, just smart, and you *are* smart. You're one of the smartest people I know. One letter from your lawyers and I would have handed over the money for you to buy yourself a decent place to live. You didn't have to return to that shithole.'

'That shithole is my home,' she reminded him. 'It's the only home I've ever known.'

The breath of his sigh danced into her hair. 'I thought that might be the case. You were born there?'

'Technically, I was born in a hospital, but yes, I've always lived there, and I know it's gone to the dogs in recent years, but it wasn't always like that. When I was growing up, there was a real sense of community about the place. Everyone looked out for everyone.'

'But in your flat, it was just you and your parents?'

'Only until I was ten, and then it was just me and Mum.'

'I never did ask you how she died, did I?' There was a sadness in his voice as he said this.

'No.' Until the last week, Marnie's past had never come up in conversation between them.

'I'm sorry for that. I should have asked.'

'It's okay. I've never really liked talking about my parents.'

'So how did she die? Was it cancer?'

'No. Cirrhosis of the liver.' She felt his body tense. 'My mother was an alcoholic. She basically pickled herself to death.'

He exhaled a drawn-out oath.

'It's why my father left. She drank all the time. I mean, *all* the time, and she was a mean drunk. I don't remember my father being an alcoholic, but his behaviour wasn't much better. They were always fighting and screaming at each other. The neighbours were always banging on the walls for them to shut up. It was a very abusive relationship.'

'Why didn't he take you with him when he left?'

'I don't know. I haven't seen him since he walked out.'

He swore again. 'He left you with an abusive alcoholic?'

'She never abused me. Half the time, she didn't even notice I was there. I think Dad waited until I was old enough to fend for myself before packing his bags.'

'At ten?' Disbelief resonated in his voice.

'I could cook by then—we were taught simple dishes at school. He knew I wouldn't starve. I'd also perfected the art of forging Mum's signature and could access her phone for anything that needed to be done digitally. Once he'd gone, I ordered food deliveries every week, and when I needed something like a new school uniform, I would just order it online too. Mum must have known what I was doing, but she never cared. As long as she had her vodka, she didn't care what I was doing.'

'And where did the money to pay for it all come from? I assume she wasn't working?'

'Benefits. The flat was paid off so she had little in the way of overheads.'

'She owned the flat?'

'Yes. She inherited it from her father before I was born. Don't ask me where her mother was. I never met her. From the little my mother told me about her family, they were a bunch of drunks too.' A bunch of drunks who'd had no interest in meeting Marnie. A whole family she'd never met, as invisible to them as she was to her mother and as forgotten by them as she was by her father.

'Have you tried to trace any of them? Or trace your father?' he asked quietly.

'Why would I? If they wanted me in their lives, I would be in their lives. As for my father, he chose to cut me from his life. I know he only stayed as long as he did for my sake, but he could have taken me with him. He could have checked that I was okay. I'm sure he's got his reasons for turning his back on me, but I don't care what they are. Not now. I feel our baby move inside me, and I feel such love in my heart for it that it hurts to breathe. I would never abandon it or do anything to harm it.'

Her father had never felt that love for Marnie. He'd done his duty by her for as long as he could endure and then left with no forwarding address. The only person in her life who'd ever seen her as a whole person and valued her was the man whose arms were wrapped around her.

Domenico kissed the top of her head and tightened the wrap of his arms around her.

With wistfulness rising in her, Marnie quietly continued. 'I know my mother must have felt a similar love for me when she was pregnant because she managed to cut down on her drinking. I was able to access my health records when I turned eighteen, and I learned I was evaluated for foetal alcohol syndrome when I was a toddler. I'd had no idea…' She closed her eyes, trying to capture an image of her mother sober. Nothing came. 'That she had me tested means she was already an alcoholic when I was conceived. That I was given the all-clear means she didn't drink enough to harm me when she was pregnant—it means she managed to control it for my sake.' It meant, Marnie suddenly realised, that had mother *had* loved her. Had truly loved her. That Marnie hadn't just been this child living in the same flat as her. Her mother had loved her as much as her disease would allow. She'd loved her from conception and had held on to life until Marnie had been old enough to go out into the world as an adult.

She'd never looked at it that way before.

She could feel Domenico's heart thudding against her back. Could hear the heaviness of his breathing, and remembered how he'd said he wanted to know her history so he could understand what drove her. What he would take from her story, she didn't know, but speaking it aloud for the first time was giving her so much of a fresh perspective on it all that it felt like she'd always looked at her past and recent history through a murky lens that was now suddenly clearing. Pieces of the jigsaw puzzle that was her life were slotting into place, and those pieces were brightly coloured.

Her own heart starting to thud, Marnie twisted her head and kissed his shoulder. 'The water's getting cold,' she said softly.

CHAPTER TWELVE

When they left the bathroom, it was still dark outside. Domenico knew it wouldn't be long until the sun began to rise. They needed to sleep.

But when he lay down and spooned himself to Marnie, sleep still felt very far away.

He could not get her story out of his mind. It filled every crevice of his brain.

He'd long ago intuited that her childhood had been far from the idyllic one he'd enjoyed, but he'd never imagined it was that far removed. Left and possibly forgotten by her father, invisible to her alcoholic mother, Marnie had essentially raised herself.

Knowing from the way she was breathing that she was still awake too, he said, 'Were you still at school when your mother died?'

'Only just. She died a month before my first A-level exam. I'd turned eighteen a few months before that.'

An answer that made him feel sick to the pit of his stomach. 'How were you able to get such good grades?' Good? Curiosity had driven him to read Marnie's file years ago. She'd earned straight As.

'Studying was my escapism.' She wriggled out of his

hold and rolled onto her back. Through the dawn starting to filter through the drapes, he could see her eyes were open, her gaze fixed on the ceiling. 'My grades were the one thing that was entirely in my hands. I wasn't even thinking about them for my future, just for the now, because I always assumed my future would be me taking care of Mum. When she died…' Her slender throat moved as she swallowed. 'I always knew she'd die early, but when it happened… It was devastating. She was a terrible mother, but she was *my* mother, and I loved her, and suddenly she was gone, and I was all alone in the world, and that was terrifying, so I did what I've always done and concentrated on what I could control, which was my exams. I also had to deal with my mother's estate, which wasn't easy, but it gave me something else to focus on, and it turned out I was good at it.'

She turned her head to him and gave a small smile. 'It was dealing with Mum's probate that made me think of a career in law. It was the first time I'd ever thought of a career for myself. I'd planned to get a job waitressing or something like it, just to pay the bills, but I started searching for jobs in law firms that only required A levels, and found the advert for a receptionist at Cannavaro Law International. I applied the day I took my final exam, and the rest is history.'

The sickness in Domenico's stomach had spread; risen all the way up his throat. He had to clear it to hoarsely say, 'That was a lucky day for Cannavaro Law.'

'It was a lucky day for me.' She twisted onto her

side and nuzzled her face close to his. 'You have no idea what your praise and belief in me meant to me. The way you took me under your wing…' She palmed his cheek. 'I was desperately lonely and ripe for falling in love, and there you were, this powerful, successful, drop-dead gorgeous man who saw something in me that no one else had seen before…' Her shoulders rose and fell in a sigh. 'I made you my life. If you'd told me to throw myself in front of a train for you, I would have done it without question.' She sighed again, her chin wobbling. 'And then you asked me to marry you.' She swallowed, then whispered, 'It took a long, long time for me to accept that the marriage you wanted was nothing like the marriage I'd dreamed of for us…' She smiled tremulously. 'I dreamed of you proposing to me every night from the day I met you.'

The image of Marnie as she'd been as a fresh-faced eighteen-year-old flashed in his mind. She'd been so *young.*

He'd become aware of her crush as the years had passed, much in the same way he was aware of the weather. It just was. A fact of life that didn't merit talking about. He'd had no idea it had set root that early.

'Instead of telling you how unhappy I was, I retreated further into my shell, just like I did when I was a little girl,' she continued quietly. 'When my parents' arguments escalated and I became frightened, I would hide in my wardrobe with my hands over my ears. I guess my childish reasoning was that if I couldn't see or hear them, it wasn't happening, and that's what I did with you. I never learned how to manage confrontation.'

Blood pounded in Domenico's ears as he envisaged the little girl in the photo hiding in a dark wardrobe, covering her ears tightly and blocking out the world. 'You were scared of me?'

'Never.' She rubbed her thumb over his jawline and gave another tremulous smile that turned into a wide yawn. 'It's just how I'd learned to cope with bad stuff. Hide and pretend and hope it goes away.'

Shuddering a breath out of his tight lungs, he pulled her into his arms so her head was on his chest, and held her tightly.

The soft warmth of her skin on his gave the comfort he craved, but did little to dispel the nausea raging through him.

After the longest time had passed, he quietly said, 'When you said in the rose garden that you'd wanted rescuing from your life… I think I understand now what you meant.'

'It was the loneliness that was the worst.' Exhaustion now made her voice barely audible. 'Working for you made me stronger and happier and more confident in myself, but then I'd go home and feel like a lost little girl again. I learned to cope and find ways through it, but sometimes…' Her voice tailed off, but he already knew what she would have said. That sometimes her loneliness had been more than she could bear.

He could hardly bring himself to ask. 'Were you very lonely in our marriage?'

She took such a long time to answer that he thought

she'd fallen asleep. When she did finally answer, he wished she had. Sleepiness etched into every syllable, she whispered, 'It's the loneliest I've ever been. When I married you, I lost you.'

After a few hours of sleep coming only in snatches, Domenico gave up. Marnie was sleeping peacefully, nestled beside him, an arm slung over his waist. When he carefully moved it off him, she rolled over and burrowed deeper beneath the sheets. She was in the exact same position when he'd finished showering and dressing.

His heart the heaviest he'd ever known it, he pressed a kiss to her temple and slipped downstairs.

Stomach too tight for food, he asked for black coffee to be served in his home office. There, he settled at his desk, turned his computer on, and began searching. He knew exactly where to start his search, but it took three cups of strong coffee before he knew it was time to stop.

He'd hoped to find evidence that Marnie's father had died. Hoped he'd be able to tell her that when he'd walked out on her mother, he hadn't walked out on Marnie too, that he'd met an unfortunate accident with a bus or suffered an aneurysm. Anything would have been preferable to the truth that her father was alive and living only half a mile from the flat he'd abandoned her in.

Scraping his fingers through his hair, Domenico drew in a ragged breath.

Marnie's father *had* abandoned her. She'd been right

not to want to track him down. Peter Ware was now as great an alcoholic as the woman who'd born his only child. How he was still alive was one of life's great mysteries.

Another of life's great mysteries was how the hell those two selfish degenerates had produced a child like Marnie. The biggest mystery of all was how the hell Marnie hadn't turned out like them. She'd defied all the odds. Defied them without any help. Taken her life into her own hands.

The strength and fortitude it must have taken for her to do that. And all without any bitterness at the hand life had dealt her. Quiet anger towards her father for his abandonment, quiet sadness and attempted understanding for everything else she'd gone through.

Dio, if that had been him, he'd have wreaked vengeance on *everyone* and laid a trail of fire in his wake.

But vengeance wasn't Marnie's way. Not against her father for abandoning her, not against her alcoholic mother who'd abandoned her in a different way, and not against her husband for being so monstrously selfish he made her parents seem like amateurs in the selfish leagues.

Domenico had treated her worse than anyone.

No wonder she hadn't wanted to come back to him.

Dio, how could she even look him in the eye without wanting to stab a knife into his heart?

Rubbing his eyes, he swallowed in an effort to keep down the coffee he'd drunk. But even the guilt-nausea ravaging him made him think of Marnie and how she'd taken her sickness—severe sickness—so stoically. Not a single word of complaint of the new hand life had dealt her. Probably because she'd learned at a young age to take care of herself during sickness, just as she'd had to take care of herself in every other way. It was the only time Domenico had stepped up to the mark and taken care of her the way she deserved, and even then it had primarily been because she was carrying his child.

She'd dreamed of a fairy tale. He'd given her a nightmare and expected her to be grateful for it. He'd not even had the decency to give her a fairy-tale wedding, and as he thought this, he closed his eyes, remembering the photos of their 'big day' his brother-in-law had taken. Domenico hadn't even bothered to hire a professional photographer for it, and when Gio had emailed the photos to him, he'd flicked through them only cursorily.

He hadn't wanted to see what they showed.

Taking a deep breath, he searched on his desktop for the folder and opened it.

He scrolled through them, one by one. The perfunctory kiss to seal the marriage in the registry office, so perfunctory their lips had hardly touched. No pictures of them being strewn in confetti because there hadn't been any confetti. The bride's pretty white dress had remained untouched.

Only a handful of 'official' pictures in the pretty garden of the manor house they'd dined at, all at his mother's insistence. All group shots. The bride and groom and the groom's family. None of the bride's family because she didn't have a family, and the groom had been too fucking selfish to care.

And then he reached the photo he'd barely let his eyes glance at before, but which he must have soaked in and retained in some part of him because the beats of his heart had become even weightier the closer he'd got to it.

The photo was of Domenico's mother and sister sitting at a bench table in the garden, smoking. Despite being a non-smoker, Marnie had gone out with them, probably at his mother's insistence. His mother and sister were talking animatedly, Marnie seemingly listening and smiling along with them. It was only when you zoomed in that the sense of something being wrong crystallised into something concrete. Marnie's gaze was far away, not just off into the distance but somewhere else completely. The deep grey of her eyes the lens had captured was filled with abject misery.

He'd been the cause of that misery. Him. His monstrous selfishness had trapped the purest heart into a loveless marriage. He'd never allowed himself to see her as fully human, never allowed himself to care about her needs or wishes or even ask what they were. And he was still doing it, he realised, utterly sickened with himself. Marnie had told him she had no wish to trace her father, and he'd disregarded that wish. It didn't matter that his intentions had been good; he'd still ignored her wishes.

She deserved so much more. Deserved so much better.

Marnie deserved so much better than him.

Domenico had no idea how long he gazed at that heartbreaking photo, but by the time he finally blinked his stare away, he knew what he had to do.

To Marnie's disappointment, she woke to an empty bed. And then she noticed the time and smiled. No wonder Domenico was already up—it was gone lunch!

Stretching, she climbed out of bed and padded over to the tray of food that had been placed on the coffee table for her. Though she really did seem to be over the sickness, Domenico's staff still liked to ensure fresh food of all varieties was available to her at all times so she could eat little and often as she'd done when she'd been in full-blown recovery mode. She guessed this would be the second tray of food brought in to her that day.

Lifting the silver lid, she found paninis still warm in their foil wrapping, bowls of nuts and an abundance of fruit.

After eating a banana slowly, followed by a handful of almonds and a glass of water, she took a shower and then put on one of her favourite summer dresses and a thin cardigan. The skies outside were blue, but she'd noticed the chill of autumn starting to penetrate the heat these last few days.

Let the seasons change, she thought dreamily. Her season had changed, so why not the world around her?

It felt like her heart had changed from winter to spring overnight. The most beautiful night of her life.

She felt somehow purged. The fresh perspectives talking over her past with Domenico had given her had freed something inside her. She'd felt a brand-new lightness in the bath with him, and now she felt it from the tips of her toes to the roots of her hair, like she'd shed something dark and frightening she hadn't even known lived inside her, and now she could embrace the world with brightness and hope and love.

She wanted to embrace this brand-new world with Domenico.

Downstairs, Marnie searched the plentiful ancient rooms for Domenico, eventually finding him in his office. It was a room she'd not entered since their marriage. Nothing had changed since then. It was still all dark wood panelling and dark furniture countered by the light pouring in through the abundance of sash windows. Stacks of Italian legal tomes lined the walls. It was the most homely of his home offices and the one she'd been happiest working alongside him in. She still missed those days.

'Your week off from work is going well, I see,' she teased lightly as she crossed the threshold. 'If you can drag yourself away from your desktop, do you fancy exploring the secret garden with me?'

He looked up from his desktop and gave a wan smile that didn't meet his eyes.

'Is something wrong?' He looked exhausted, and, remembering why he must be so tired, she smiled. Oh, but she felt all giddy and light inside, and she leaned down to kiss him and infuse some of her lightness into him. Their lips made only minimal contact before he gripped her hips to stop her getting any closer.

Light brown eyes locked onto hers. There was none of the sensuous gleam in them that she'd anticipated after a night like they'd just shared, and suddenly she felt a pang of alarm.

'Marnie…' His throat moved. 'We need to talk,'

The alarm growing, she reached her hands into his hair and threaded her fingers through the soft strands. Oh, it felt incredible to be able to do this. To just be able to touch him and know her touch was wanted. 'What's happened?'

He closed his eyes briefly. 'Please, sit down.'

Thinking it an invitation to sit on his lap, she did just that, only to find him stiffening, and not in a sexual way. She twisted a little so she could see his face more clearly and palmed his cheek. 'Dom?'

The strong throat moved again before he captured the hand on his cheek and gazed into her eyes. 'Marnie, it's time for me to let you go.'

Confounded, she looked even deeper into his eyes. 'Go where?'

'Wherever you want.' He shook his head and gently moved her hand from his face. 'I'm doing what I should have done a long time ago and setting you free.'

A piercing sound began ringing in her ears. 'What are you talking about?'

Lips tightening, his chest rose sharply. 'I should have let you go when you served the divorce papers on me.'

At her blank stare…blank because she just could not comprehend what he was talking about, he said, 'When you served the divorce papers on me, I should have taken your decision with good grace—the kind of grace you would have shown if the positions had been reversed. Instead, I fought you every inch of the way. I fought dirty, and when you got pregnant, I fought even dirtier. I used your illness to my advantage. I moved you back under my roof with the false promise that I would accept you were not coming back to me. I never intended to keep that promise.'

The piercing sound in her ears was becoming louder by the second. She swallowed moisture into a throat that had gone suddenly dry, and whispered, 'I know that.'

She'd always known, and he'd always known that she knew that particular promise had been a lie. What she didn't know was why it sounded like he was saying he wanted her to leave. The ringing in her ears must be preventing her from listening to him properly because he couldn't be saying what her increasingly clammy hands and painfully beating heart were telling her he was saying. It wasn't possible. You didn't have the kind of loving intimacy they'd finally found together and then push it away.

'You know it because you know the kind of man I am,' he said steadily, not breaking the lock of their eyes. 'You know *me*, Marnie, better than anyone. And now I know you, too. You know I am selfish and arrogant and will stop at nothing to get what I want, and I know you deserve a hell of a lot better than me. You deserve better than a man who took advantage of the fragile heart he knew had been freely given to him and treated it with contempt. You deserve better than the man who stole your dreams and destroyed them for his own selfish needs. I treated you like you were put on this earth to fulfil my needs, and now I need to let you go so you can fulfil *your* needs. You have never lived your life for yourself, *cuoricina*. You deserve the freedom to make the choices that are right for you and live your life on your own terms, and this is the only way I can give it to you.'

Holding on to his stare for dear life because now the room was starting to spin, Marnie had to fight to open her closed throat and say, 'What if I want my freedom to be with you?'

'How could you want that after everything I've done to you?' he asked with a pained groan before shaking his head. 'This is the only way I can take my penance for all that I have done to you. I have to let you go, Marnie. You deserve happiness and freedom, and I deserve the hell of purgatory without you in my life. I've transferred a sum of money into your bank account that is the amount I should have given you when we divorced, and I've set about transferring the London house into your name.'

Throat now fully closed, she shook her head, pleading mutely with her eyes for him to *just stop talking*.

His smile sad, he rubbed a finger the length of her cheek. 'I know you've never wanted my money, but you will need it, and you will need a decent place to live and raise our child. I understand you will probably want to keep your flat for sentimentality's sake, but you know our child deserves to be brought up in wealth and safety. I will arrange for my jet to take you home this afternoon and arrange for my personal possessions to be moved out before you arrive. Consider it yours as of now. I will get my team to draw up a contract for maintenance for you and the baby. We can deal with visitation rights in it. Primary custody will be yours if that's what you want, or we can share custody. Whatever you want, however you want to do it, I will be guided by you and abide by your wishes.'

'Can you hear yourself?' she whispered, the words she had to fight to get out almost strangled.

'Yes. I'm doing what I should have done a long time ago.'

'No, you're not.' Clambering off his lap, her legs were shaking so hard that she had to lean against his desk to remain upright. Drawing all the strength she could muster into her voice, she looked him dead in the eye. 'You're doing what you've always done—what's best for *you*.'

His flinch almost made her laugh. Maybe she would have laughed if she wasn't trembling from her fight to control the tears pleading for release.

She couldn't believe this was happening. After the closeness they'd found, the love they'd found—and it *had* been love, she knew it, and would never let herself believe she'd imagined what they'd shared and what she'd felt in his kisses and seen in his eyes—he was slamming the door on them.

'Everything has always been about you and what you need, and it still is,' she choked out. 'Your conscience over your treatment of me has finally caught up with you, and so you've unilaterally decided to gift me my freedom and give me primary custody of our child as a form of penance to salve it. How very magnanimous of you, and how very Domenico to make me fall in love with you again and then drop me from a great height, and then pretend it's for my benefit. Do you even believe that? After last night?'

Now she did laugh, even as the tears finally spilled over, as the truth of his actions slapped her across the face.

'But of *course* it's about last night,' she despaired. 'This is you all over. You want to control everything, even what lies in our hearts.' She wiped the tears away with the sleeve of her cardigan, but it did nothing to stem the flow. At least she couldn't see his face clearly through the tears. At least she wasn't forced to suffer the expression on his face and read the truth she knew would be resonating on it. 'You'll never let yourself love me, will you? Not properly. Not with the whole of your heart. It's so much easier to push me away than get tied up in all those messy *hot and passionate* emotions that only Carmela was allowed before she broke you.'

'Goddamnit, Marnie, this has *nothing* to do with her. I'm doing this for *you*, don't you see that, and I'm doing it for you because—'

'No, you're doing it for *you*,' she interrupted, her voice cracking even as it rose in pain-filled anger. 'Did you consider for a minute what I want? Did it cross your mind for a second to ask if I even wanted my freedom from you? No, because it was never about me. If it had been, you'd have known that I'd already forgiven you for the past. I'd forgiven you because of my own part in it, for failing to find my voice and keeping everything bottled up—you made me see that. It was never just you, Dom. It was both of us, but you don't want an us, not in the way I do, because if you'd asked me, I would have told you the only future I want is with you, and now it's too late. I forgave you the past, but I will never forgive you for this. You want me out of your life—consider your wish granted.'

CHAPTER THIRTEEN

DOMENICO WATCHED MARNIE speed-walk out of his office with the sensation that he'd just been hit by a truck.

What the *hell* had just happened?

He tried to think, but his mind was reeling as he tried to make sense of it all, especially Marnie's upset at being given the freedom she'd wanted for so long. Why hadn't she snatched it out of his hands…?

The force of another truck slammed into him.

He'd done it *again*, he despaired.

In his desperation to make things right, he'd failed to ask what she wanted and taken the choice out of her hands, and as this thought impacted him, another truck smashed into him, this one right in the solar plexus.

How very Domenico to make me fall in love with you again…

He blinked hard and straightened, his thrumming heart now competing with his reeling mind to stop him from thinking straight. That had to be a false memory, surely? How could she possibly have fallen in love with him after everything he'd done to her…?

More memories flowed, jumbled and scattered, all of them Marnie's chameleon eyes, the only part of her where the truth always shone if you only opened your own eyes to see it.

She'd glided into his office with love shining out of them. Love for him.

Marnie *loved* him. She loved him, and…

A cold sweat broke out on his back as he replayed their conversation from her perspective; from the perspective of a woman who'd only ever known rejection from those she loved.

Pulling himself to his feet, he set off after her at a run.

Marnie didn't know where she was walking to, had no destination in mind, knew only that she had to keep walking to keep her heart pumping and her lungs inflating and deflating because if she stopped the tight pain in her chest would engulf them.

She couldn't fall apart. She mustn't. She had to think of her baby, but oh God, oh God, the *pain.*

She'd barely registered passing the maze when she saw the chapel ahead of her. Marnie had been to church only a handful of times in her life. Each of those times had been in primary school for the compulsory Christmas Christingle service. She remembered feeling cold on her skin but warm in her heart in those services. It had been such a lovely, comforting feeling that she'd taken herself to the last two services after her dad had left and her mum had been in no state to take her. It was the first time Marnie had forged her signature on a permission slip.

Now, she felt the opposite of how she'd felt in those

services, and she picked up speed, suddenly longing to feel a glimmer of that long-ago warmth and comfort.

To her despair, the door was closed.

Frightened at how close she was to screaming her pain, she stumbled to the stone wall behind it and found the wall-high door, mostly hidden by thick foliage from the hedge running the length of the wall. It was the door that opened into the secret garden. It was so long since it had last been used that the doorknob was reluctant to turn, but eventually it did, and she had to push against the door with her arm while turning it to get it to open.

Stepping inside, she took a deep breath and cast her stare around, momentarily struck by the jumble of late-blooming flowers and cascades of foliage running wild. The sweetness she breathed in was soothing enough for her to take more deep breaths as she gazed at what had once been a hidden paradise filled with stone arches, water fountains and snaking pathways.

All that was left were the ruins. Nature had taken control of the man-made order and given beautiful chaos, like something from a fairy tale.

A short walk inside, she found a stone bench. After wiping it with her cardigan's sleeve, she sat down and closed her eyes.

Maybe it was better to be here amongst the ruins of a fallen paradise than in the chapel. It felt more fitting. She understood nature better than she did the teachings of the church. She'd tried very hard to bring nature into her flat, and she suddenly remembered Domenico presenting her with a box of the cherry tomatoes she'd grown after he'd gone to collect her clothes.

He couldn't have known the care and attention she'd given the little seedlings she'd germinated to turn into healthy, productive plants. He could have ignored them. Instead, he'd taken the time to pick them for her, and because she'd been too ill to eat them, he'd had his chef preserve them for when she was better.

His face swam before her.

Tears fell down her face.

What a fool she'd been to let him get so close when she knew he still had the power to hurt her, and what a bigger fool to have believed she had the power to control her reactions to it.

'I'm sorry,' she whispered tearfully to her baby, rubbing her belly. 'I did try. I think your daddy did too, but…'

She couldn't bring herself to tell her baby that its daddy didn't want to love its mummy.

And that was the worst of it. That she'd finally felt his love. He'd felt her love too, and rejected her for it…

A stray thought suddenly made her blink and straighten, but by the time she'd brushed away the tears with her grubby fingers, it had vanished.

But her heart was pounding, her pulse racing.

What had she been thinking before the stray thought had come into her head? About Domenico rejecting her love, that was it, and the stray thought leapt back at her.

With hot blood zooming between her ears, Marnie thought harder than she'd ever done before, trying to remember every word he'd said and every expression in his eyes before the tears had fallen too hard for her to see them.

He'd offered her custody of their baby. That's what the stray thought had been. The man who wouldn't entertain the thought of being a part-time father had put their child's entire future in her hands, and he'd *meant* it.

He'd meant it because he loved her.

The very act of letting her go—and letting their baby go—was an act of love. The greatest act of love he could have given her.

She looked again at the beautiful chaos surrounding her and stumbled to her feet.

Wasn't this what their baby represented? Domenico had tried to impose man-made order on their marriage, but it had needed the beautiful chaos of emotions—real emotions—to create their baby. That bitter fury that had driven them both the night they'd conceived their child *had* come from emotion. It had come from the desperate unhappiness they'd both been feeling at the loss of the other.

She hurried to the door, a smile breaking out over her face.

He did love her. He did! And he wasn't the one hiding from it, not this time. This time it was all Marnie, frightened, lonely Marnie, because over the last few months she'd fallen in love with him for real, not as a fantasy figure in a fairy tale but as a flesh and blood man, and all she knew of real love was rejection. When he'd said he was giving her freedom, she'd heard that he didn't want her anymore, because that's what she'd expected to hear, because that's what she knew. Rejection.

Domenico hadn't been rejecting her love; he'd been showing her his.

He *loved* her!

Almost fizzing with revelation, she put her hand on the doorknob and twisted it…only for it to come off in her hand.

Where the hell was she?

Domenico and his staff had searched every inch of the villa and its grounds. They'd checked the security cameras that covered the whole perimeter of his estate. Nothing. It was like Marnie had vanished into thin air.

She'd been gone for six hours, and the only thing he knew for certain was that she hadn't left the estate.

So where the hell was she?

Smacking his palm to his forehead, he commanded himself to think. She had to be somewhere. People didn't just vanish. People like Marnie especially didn't just vanish. Not his calm, thoughtful wife.

But she'd been so distraught.

Dio, how could she believe he didn't love her? Didn't she know by now that he couldn't live without her? He'd thought letting her go was the best thing for her, the one act of love he could give the woman who'd been through so much, and so much of it at his selfish hands.

A memory floated in his frantic mind of the wine she'd been drinking when he'd arrived at her door the night they conceived their child. The woman with alcoholic parents who never drank, not even a glass of champagne on their wedding day. He could not begin to the imagine the depth of her misery for her to have taken that step…

Her misery had been of the same depth as his own, although whether it was because she'd still held residual love for him or because the decree nisi had made the termination of them so final, he didn't know.

But her beautiful, damaged heart had fallen in love with him again, that much he did know, and she was out there somewhere believing he'd rejected it.

The panic he'd been barely containing set in.

Where was she? Her phone was in the bedroom, and as far as he knew, she had no food or water.

It suddenly came to him. The one place they hadn't looked. The place she'd mentioned when she'd come so happily into his office. He'd been so full of anguish at what he was about to do that he'd barely heard her.

If you can drag yourself away from your desktop, do you fancy exploring the secret garden with me?

Snatching at the bottle of water he'd been carrying around for when he found her, Domenico headed back into the grounds and ran past the maze at the fastest pace of his life.

Marnie was all cried out. She'd heard the voices calling her name, but they hadn't got close enough to her to hear her shouts back, not with all the thick foliage surrounding her muffling her voice. That's what had set the tears off. More frustration than fear.

The autumn air was getting chilly, and she tried not to think about it, just as she tried not to think that she hadn't drunk anything since the glass of water when she'd woken. If she didn't have such personal experience of how long a pregnant woman could go without water before it affected her baby, that would be the one thing to get her panicking.

Domenico would find her. Of that, she had absolute faith.

It was just that as her thirst and the chill in the air increased and the sun began to set, the thought of being trapped in here for any length of time in the dark…

She concentrated on breathing.

If she let the fear out, then panic would set in.

The shadows were getting very long, though. Frighteningly long. There was a tree a short distance away from her that had to be fifty feet high. The shadows of its branches danced in front of her like groping fingers.

She drew her knees to her chest and hugged herself. Her bottom was numb from the cold of the stone bench, and her feet were freezing.

The shadows were coming even closer.

'Marnie!'

Her heart thumped. She lifted her head, hardly daring to believe she'd just heard her name, and so close too, and then she heard a loud slam and a door swinging open and footsteps crunching.

'Marnie! Where are you?'

'I'm right here!' she called back, although her throat was so dry and hoarse from thirst and shouting that it was more of a croak than words. She'd barely made it to her feet when he emerged from the shadows.

There was no hesitation. One moment he was five

feet away from her; the next he'd lifted her into his arms and was carrying her out of the secret garden's door.

Only when he reached the chapel did he speak, sitting down on a wooden bench beside it and keeping her firmly on his lap while thrusting a bottle of water in her hand. 'Drink.'

She obeyed. Drinking slowly, she gazed through the romantic night lights that glowed around them at the beautiful face of the only man she would ever love, her heart filled with an emotion so true and pure that all she could do was carry on staring.

And he was staring right back with the same expression she knew was ringing from her eyes.

When she passed the bottle to him to share, their fingers brushed.

His eyes widened. '*Dio*, you're freezing.' In moments, he'd stripped his shirt off and draped it over her, all the while not letting her move an inch off his lap. Once satisfied he'd wrapped the shirt around every available inch of her body, he pulled his phone out of his back pocket and made a quick call, and then she was swooping back through the air as he stood back up, carrying her up with him.

Adjusting his hold to secure her to him, he glowered down at her. 'Don't you ever put me through that again.'

If Marnie hadn't already known he loved her, the way Domenico's voice broke on the last syllable and tears filled his eyes would have confirmed it, and she pressed her cheek to his naked chest and closed her eyes. 'I'm sorry,' she whispered. 'Sorry for what I said and sorry for scaring you.'

He didn't respond verbally, just pressed a tight kiss to the top of her head and then set off again.

In the warmth of the villa, he headed straight up the stairs, only putting her down when they reached the bedroom, where he set her down gently on the bed. The delicious scent of fresh bubble bath permeated the room.

As docile as a lamb, Marnie let him strip her naked and then carry her into the bathroom. There, he held her hand tightly as she stepped into the steaming, foamy water. Once she was lying back in it and her cold body was sighing with relief at the warmth enveloping it, she watched him strip his trousers and underwear off.

He stepped into the water and settled on the other side of it to her, holding her stare. His features tight, his eyes glittering, he said, 'Let me make one thing very clear. My marriage to Carmela was a nightmare. We were completely wrong for each other and made each other damned miserable. Yes, we had passion to start with, but there was nothing to underpin it, not from either of us. I never contested the divorce or tried to win her back. She came to me months after she left and tried to seduce me into trying again, but there was nothing left in me for her. I felt *nothing*, not on any kind of emotional level. All those years of my vengeance was for my pride, not for her. I never wanted her back, but you, *fiore mio*...'

With a shuddering sigh, he shook his head and

pushed himself forward, kneeling between her legs. Bringing his face close to hers, he whispered, 'When you left me… I went out of my mind.'

Her heart ballooned to the sky at the admission.

'What I felt for Carmela is the difference between a pebble and a mountain compared to how I feel for you. With you, the passion is different and so much more because it's entwined and underpinned by love. You said before that you'd made me your life…well, that's how I feel for you, because *you* are my life. I don't know when I fell in love with you, but it feels like I've loved you forever, and when you love someone, truly love them, then all that matters is their happiness, and that's all that matters to me. Your happiness. That's what I thought I was giving to you earlier.' Gently, he traced the contours of her ear. 'You, *fiore mio*, are more deserving of happiness and the joy life can give than anyone else in this world, and if you feel you can give me the chance to be the one to share that happiness with, then you will make me the happiest man in this world.

'Please, Marnie, let me share my life with you, not for our baby's sake but for *our* sake, because we love each other and because I can't live without you. I swear I will spend the rest of my life making up for all the…'

She silenced his mouth with a finger to his lips. 'That's already in the past,' she whispered with a smile. 'Don't you already know you're the only person in the world who's ever made me happy? I've loved you forever, Domenico Cannavaro, and I will love you forever.'

His chest rising, he blew out an exhalation and lifted

his chest upright, out of the water. Taking her left hand, he rubbed her ring finger and gazed deep into her eyes. 'Marnie Ware, will you do me the honour of my life and marry me?'

She didn't have to think twice about it. 'Yes.'

'Yes?'

'*Yes*. Yes, love of my life, I will marry you.'

In a beat, giant hands had captured her face, and then she was being devoured by kisses so hot and passionate that they smothered all the ghosts of the past, starving them so completely that by the time they came up for air, the ghosts had vanished for good.

EPILOGUE

DOMENICO SAT IN the home office he shared with his wife in their Roman villa, looking for perhaps the hundredth time through their wedding photos. The professional photographer he'd hired had captured every beautiful minute of it.

Domenico had wanted their nuptials to take place in a cathedral, but Marnie had wanted the chapel of the villa they'd made their home, and so, of course, he'd given in and let her have her way, even though it had meant having to cut the prospective guest list by two-thirds. He'd let her have her way over the whole of it, as he did about pretty much everything in their lives. A happy wife made for a happy life, and Domenico's life was blissful.

His favourite photo was the one taken on the grounds after the service, of the two of them and six-month-old Luca. He had Luca in his arms, and Marnie was gazing at them both with open adoration. Not a single photo of their wedding day showed her as anything but blissfully happy. It was all there in her eyes, shining as blue that day as the sky that had covered them.

Her eyes always shone. He knew his eyes did, too.

'There you are.'

He looked up from his desk to find Marnie slipping into the office, beautiful in a strapless, light blue dress that fell to her knees. She closed the door behind her.

He held out his arms to her. She curled onto his lap and, after a loving kiss, pressed her cheek to his and saw what he was looking at. 'Again?' she teased.

He grinned and kissed her, and then, because he could never resist—never *wanted* to resist—kissed her again. 'Are the children asleep?' he asked huskily, slipping his hand up the skirt of her dress.

Her eyes gleamed. 'Fast asleep.'

'Georgina?' Their live-in nanny who had to be the most underused and overpaid nanny in existence.

'Watching one of her reality shows.'

'Excellent.' He skimmed his fingers higher.

'We've got a table booked,' she reminded him, even as she worked on the belt of his trousers.

'They'll wait for us.'

She grinned, and jumped to her feet. 'Of course they will.' In seconds, she'd pulled her knickers off and stepped out of them. Seconds later, she was back on his lap, this time straddling him. She put her mouth to his and whispered, 'Happy wedding anniversary, husband.'

'Happy wedding anniversary…' he groaned as she sank on his hard length '…wife.'

* * * * *

Did Enemies with Consequences *leave you wanting more? Then you're certain to love these other dramatic stories from Michelle Smart!*

Spaniard's Shock Heirs
Forgotten Greek Proposal
His Pregnant Enemy Bride
Greek Boss to Hate
Marriage Made in Revenge

Available now!